PRETTY WHEN YOU CRY

SKYE WARREN

And the day came when the risk to remain tight in a bud was more painful than the risk it took to blossom.

–Anaïs Nin

CHAPTER ONE

S O FAR, A city looks exactly how I thought it would—gutted buildings and dark alleys.

A den of wickedness.

This morning I woke up on my floor mat in Harmony Hills. Sunlight streamed through the window while dust rose up to meet it. The white walls somehow kept their color despite rough dirt floors.

A desperate trek through the woods and a series of bus rides later, I made it to a city. *This* city. Tanglewood. It could have been anywhere. They're all the same, all sinful, all scary—and the only thing that makes this one special is that I ran out of money for bus tickets.

My shoes are made of white canvas, already fraying and black from the grime of the streets. I made these shoes by hand when I turned twelve, and the heel on the left side has never fit quite right. But the bamboo soles lasted for years in the hills. Now they're cracking against concrete. I can feel every lump in the pavement, every loose rock, every rounded hump as the sidewalk turns to cobblestone and then back again.

That's not the worst part.

There's someone following me. Maybe more than

one person. I try to listen for the footsteps, but it's hard to hear over the pounding in my ears, the thud of my heart against my chest. Panic is a tangible force in my head, a gritty quicksand that threatens to pull me down.

I could end up on my knees before this night is over.

But I don't think I'll be saying my evening prayers.

Men are standing outside a gate that hangs open on its hinges. They fall silent as I walk close. I tighten my arms where they are folded over my chest and look down. *If I can't see them, they can't see me.* It wasn't true when I was little, and it's not true now.

One of them steps in front of me.

My breath catches, and I stop walking. My whole body is trembling by the time I meet his eyes, bloodshot red in a shadowed face. "What's your name?" he asks in a gravelly voice.

I jerk my head. *No.*

"Now that's not very polite, is it?" Another one steps closer, and then I smell him. They couldn't have showered in the past day or even week.

Cleanliness is a virtue.

Being quiet and obedient and small is a virtue too. "I'm sorry. I just want to—"

I don't know what comes next. I want to run. I want to hide. I want to pretend the past sixteen years as a disciple of the Harmony Hills never happened. None of that is possible when I'm surrounded by men. I take a step back and bump into another man. Hands close around my arms.

A sound escapes me—fear and protest. It's more than I would have done this morning, that sound.

I'm turned to face the man behind me. He smiles a broken-toothed smile. "Doesn't matter what you want, darling."

My mouth opens, but I can't scream. I can't scream because I've been taught not to. Because I know no one will come. Because the consequences of crying are worse than what will happen next.

Then the man's eyes widen in something like fear. It's a foreign expression on his face. It doesn't belong. I wouldn't even believe it except he takes a step back.

My chest squeezes tight. What's behind me? *Who* is behind me that could have inspired that kind of fear? The men surrounding me are monsters, but they're backing off now, stepping away, hands up in surrender. *No harm done,* that's what they're saying without words.

I whirl and almost slip on a loose cobblestone.

The man standing in front of me is completely still. That's the first thing I notice about him—before I see the fine cut of his black suit or the glint of a silver watch under his cuff. Before I see the expression on his face, devoid of compassion or emotion. Devoid of humanity.

"We didn't know she worked for you," one of the men mumbles.

They're still backing up, forming a circle around us, growing wider. I'm in the middle. I'm the drop, and the men around me form a ripple. Then they fade into the blackness and are gone.

It's just me and the man in the suit.

He hasn't spoken. I'm not sure he's going to. I half expect him to pull out a gun from somewhere underneath that smooth black fabric and shoot me. That's what happens in the city, isn't it? That's what everyone told me about the outside world, how dangerous it is. And even while some part of me had nodded along, had believed them, another part of me had refused.

There had to be beauty outside the white stucco walls. Beauty that wasn't contained and controlled. Beauty with color. Only apparently I was wrong. I haven't seen anything beautiful—except him.

He's beautiful in a strange and sinful way, one that makes me more afraid. Not colorful exactly. His eyes are a gray color I've never seen before, both deep and opaque at the same time. The building itself is beautiful too with its wrought iron gate around a large courtyard. The fountain in the center is broken, but that only adds to the mystique.

The marquee sign reads *Grand*, a flash of neon pink against the black night.

He steps closer, the light from the sign illuminating his face, making him look even more sinister. "What's your name?"

I couldn't answer those other men, but I find something inside for him. I find truth. "I'm not allowed to say my name to someone else."

He studies me for a long moment, taking in my tangled hair and my white dress. "Why not?"

Because God will punish me. "Because I'm running away."

He nods like this is what he expected. "Do you have money?"

I have twenty dollars left after bus fare. "Enough."

His lips twist, and I wonder if that's what a smile looks like on him. It's terrifying. "No, you don't," he says. "The question is, what would you do to earn some?"

Anything.

My voice is just a whisper. "I'm a good girl."

He laughs, and I see that I was wrong before. That wasn't a smile. It was a taunt. A challenge. This is a real smile, one with teeth. The sound rolls through me like a coming storm, deep and foreboding.

"I know," he says gently. "What's your name?"

"Candace."

He studies me. "Pretty name."

His voice is deep with promise and something else I can't decipher. All I know is he isn't really talking about my name. And I know it isn't really a compliment. "Thank you."

"Now come inside, Candace."

He turns and walks away before I can answer. I can feel the night closing in on me, the sharks in the water waiting to strike. It's not really a choice. I think the man knows that. He's counting on it. Whatever is going to happen inside will be bad, and the only thing worse is what would have happened outside.

I hurry to catch up with him, almost running across the crumbled driveway, under the marquee sign for the Grand, past the broken fountain, desperate for the dubious safety of the man who could hold the darkness at bay. It's the same thing that kept me in Harmony Hills for so long—fear and twisted gratitude.

CHAPTER TWO

HARMONY HILLS IS a place of purity, of paleness, and the city is black. Inside the building is something else entirely, an explosion of light and color. *So much color.*

The women are beautiful, skin flushed and painted and glistening with glitter. Their bodies are strong—and almost naked. Not completely. Satin straps and lace tie them up like presents as they swirl around a shiny silver pole.

No man is telling them to cover their bodies.

No man is making them sit down and be ashamed. Instead the men are looking up to them, practically panting in their eagerness, desperate for a glance or a touch, holding up money for the possibility.

I'm so enraptured by the sight of the stage that I almost lose sight of the man.

He stops in the crowd, and I see the way other men look at him—with apprehension. I see the way they move aside to let him pass. Fear whispers over my skin. The other men are panting after the girls, but not this one. He's too cold for that, too sure he can have any one of them with a snap of his fingers.

And that's what he does—snaps his fingers like I'm a stray puppy who's lost her way.

That's what I am to him.

I hurry to catch up. I get curious looks from the other patrons, but I ignore them. I'm not sexy and beautiful like the women onstage. I'm still wearing my white shift from Harmony Hills, my hair long and uneven at the bottom. We're not allowed to cut it.

There's a stairway to the side of the stage, and I follow him down. A guard of some kind waits at the bottom. His gaze flicks over me, dispassionate, as if evaluating me as a threat. I guess we both know I don't pose any, because just as quick his gaze returns straight ahead.

The room below is more basement than office, the ornate wooden desk out of place on a concrete floor. The man in the suit shuts the thick steel door, locking us in.

His footsteps echo as he crosses and sits behind the desk.

"Sit down," he tells me without even looking at me.

Sixteen years of training, of scripture ensure that I do what I'm told. I perch on the old wobbly chair in front of the desk. This room scares me. It's suited to interrogation…or torture. If that door can keep the noise out, it can hold my screams inside. No one would hear me over the thud of music anyway. And that guard waiting outside… I know without asking that he wouldn't let me leave.

I've traded one prison for another.

The man pulls out a cell phone and dials. Alarm spikes through me. "Who are you calling?" I demand, my heart beating fast.

"The police," he says, his strange gray eyes meeting mine.

Panic claws at my chest. "No," I burst out. "Don't."

One eyebrow rises. "Don't worry. I'm sure they'll give you a lollipop before they send you home."

"You can't send me back there." When I was five years old, I colored on the walls of the chapel. I had to write *I am a sinner* on my arm twenty times with a steel-tipped feather. You can still see the scar of the last *r* on my hand if I'm in the sunlight. The punishment for running away, for getting dragged back, would be much more severe.

That earns me a low laugh. "I can do anything I want with you. You seem like a smart girl. You already know that."

"Then let me stay," I whisper.

Pale eyes narrow. "Why?"

"Like those girls out there." My heart is beating out of my chest. I don't even know what I'm saying, whether I really want this or not. Whether I can even do it. "Let me work here."

Frustration flashes across his stern face, so slight I would have missed it if I wasn't staring at him—studying him. Learning him just like I learned Leader Allen for years. "Those girls," he says, his voice like ice, "are grown women. Adults. Every one of them is at least eighteen years old, because my club doesn't break the rules."

He doesn't seem like a man who follows rules, but I know what he means. He picks which rules to follow and which to break—and he has no reason to choose me.

I swallow hard. I know what's coming, I just don't know if I'll survive it. "Please."

He scans me from my loose hair to my ragged dress down to my fraying cloth slippers. "And you...well, you look all of twelve years old."

Do I really look that young? Do I really seem that innocent? "I'm eighteen," I lie.

He smiles as if we share a secret. As if we're both lying. "Of course you are. And I'm only calling the cops to protect your pretty little cunt."

I blink, the word a slap. I don't even know what it means, but I know it's bad. I know because of the harshness of the word, the hard *c* and guttural ending. I know because of the appreciation in his eyes when he says it—a man like this wouldn't like anything sweet.

He stands, and it seems like he's ten feet tall. I shrink against the wooden chair, but there's nowhere to go. "The truth is," he says, his voice smooth as water, "I'm calling the cops to get you out of my hair. And the only reason I follow the rules? Is to keep the cops from sniffing around, disrupting business. My real business. Understand?"

"Not really," I whisper.

The corner of his lip turns up. "All you need to understand is that you can't stay here. This isn't a boarding school or a sweatshop. There's no place for you here."

The words hit me harder than they should. I've only been in this building a few minutes. It should mean nothing to me. He should mean nothing to me. But it's more than this building—more than him. It's like he's speaking for the whole city. Like he's speaking for everything outside of Harmony Hills. That was the only place I've ever had, the only place I belonged. And it was going to kill me.

All the air sucks out of the basement, and I can't breathe. This is worse than torture. I'd rather he hit me than tell me I don't belong anywhere. Tears fill my eyes, making everything seem murky, underwater.

Through the haze, I see him come to stand in front of me. If he was my mother, he would hug me. If he was Leader Allen, he'd slap me.

Instead he just watches me.

He leans back against the edge of the high desk and crosses his arms. When I was a kid, there was a boy who would drop water onto an ant and watch it drown. That's how the man is looking at me—curious, as if he wants to see what will happen next.

I clench my fists, squeezing my fingernails into my skin until the physical pain is worse than the pain inside. "What's your name?" I demand, my voice shaky.

"Ivan," he says softly, still watching. Still waiting.

"Let me work here, Ivan," I say, hands clenched, body ready to fight. It's not fighting he wants from me, though. Not exactly. I may not know the word he used, but I know how he thinks. It's not that far off from the men outside who surrounded me.

It's not that far off from Leader Allen either.

I stand up and meet his gaze. "I'll do anything."

CHAPTER THREE

I KNOW WHAT will happen to me if I let him touch me. I know because every sermon I ever heard, every scripture I've ever seen promises the same thing. Eternal damnation.

That's what I'm offering him—my soul on a spit.

He doesn't look impressed. Instead he leans close, close enough that I'm forced to sit. He braces his hands on both arms of my chair. It occurs to me then how he's advanced on me since the conversation started. He was behind his desk at the beginning. He stood and circled it. Now he's inches from my face, his breath warm and soft against my forehead when he speaks.

"What could you possibly give me that I couldn't get from any one of those girls out on the floor tonight?"

My eyes shut tight. I can still see her clearly, the woman onstage. Her power in the form of bared breasts and a bold smile. She could please Ivan so much better than me, and without even asking, I know she would do whatever he wanted.

"My virginity," I whisper, trembling inside.

He's a stranger to me, but I know what he wants. He looks at me the same way Leader Allen looked at me.

That's why I had to leave. It turns out men are the same everywhere I go. They only want one thing from me.

He cocks his head. "Why would you give me that?"

With only a few dollars in my pocket and men waiting on the street outside, I don't have a choice. "I need…a place to stay."

Something dark flits over his expression. "Surely you want more than that, for something so precious."

I want freedom. I want safety, but I can't have that. "A job," I whisper.

Money is a form of freedom. Dancing and nakedness and music are freedom too.

He crouches in front of me, and something about our positions now makes me feel young. He's still holding the arms of the chair, and my hands are clenched in my lap. His eyes meet mine, but he's down low. I feel small and helpless. Trapped.

"You could ask me to pay you," he says, a strange note in his voice. It's like he's coaxing me. Like he's telling me what to do. "If I gave you enough, you'd be able to get a nice hotel room. Maybe you could keep me coming back for more."

There are too many shadows here, too many vines ready to grab me. If he paid me for sex, I'd be just like my mother. And I have no faith in my ability to keep him coming back for more. "I want to work."

He puts his hand on my knee. Just his hand. Not very high. It's an innocent touch. Any one of the elders might have touched me this way. Leader Allen definitely has.

It doesn't feel innocent. It feels dangerous, a snaking vine.

His expression is severe, but his voice is soft. It's a contradiction, just like him. "I would give you pretty jewelry and pretty clothes. My own little doll to dress up."

My breath comes faster. His words don't sound like an offer. They sound like a warning. "No."

"You'd rather fuck a hundred men than just one?"

I flinch. I'd rather keep running so that nothing can ever tie me down, no one can hold me down, ever again. "I don't want to…don't want to fu—I just want to dance."

Surprise flicks through his eyes, turning them almost silver. He draws back, considering me. He has me trapped, but he's no longer in my face. I sit very still under his regard. I have sat for hours during prayer, unable to move, unwilling. If I even stretch or look up for a second, it would prove my unworthiness. I would have to start over and face my punishment after. I can wait forever for him to decide.

"No," he says softly.

My hopes fall. If he doesn't let me stay, I'll have to go back into the streets. Fear is a cold band around my chest. *You'd rather fuck a hundred men than just one?* I might find out tonight.

Bile rises in my throat. "Wait."

"You'll come home with me. If you still want to

dance once you've had time to think about it, once *I've* had time to think about it, then we'll see."

"Oh," I whisper, something hot and scary flowing through my veins.

"And you'll do exactly as I say, whatever I decide."

His words make me cold, and I shudder. This is just like Harmony Hills, isn't it? I left there because I didn't want to live like cattle anymore, because I didn't want to be caged and bred and then shot when I was no longer useful. I shouldn't like being ordered around, not when I've risked so much to be free, but it's a wild relief to hear he has a plan for me.

My mind flashes with glitter and lace. With confidence and color. "How will I know how to please the men out there if I've never...done that?"

His eyes glow with a dark promise. "You won't please them by knowing, little one. You'll please them by *not* knowing."

"I don't understand."

A flicker, almost a smile. "Men like to teach you things. That's what gets them off."

And I know he isn't talking about the men out there. He's talking about himself.

He wants to teach me things.

The knowledge sinks inside me, imprints itself on my bones where I can't ever forget. "Okay," I whisper.

"You'll wait here for me," he says. Not a question.

I take in the dimly lit basement a little more slowly this time, from the stark lightbulb to the dark stains on the concrete floor. It's like a jail cell, and without even scripture to justify it.

Before I can answer him, he's gone. The door closes behind him with a clash of metal.

A beat passes, and then something scrapes on the other side of the door.

I'm locked inside.

Chapter Four

THERE IS NO clock inside the basement. Time passes in breaths, one after the other.

A breath to sit and stare at the closed door.

A breath to stand up.

A breath to approach the desk.

Ivan is terrifying, and I'm completely at his mercy. It's a risk to look through his stuff. It's a risk *not* to look through his stuff, now that I have the chance.

I don't know what I'm dealing with here. Why does he want me? The stories Leader Allen tells ring in my ears. The outside world is full of heathens, of sinners. It's full of violent men who want to drag me into an alley and rape me. Is that what Ivan wants?

Men like to teach you things. That's what gets them off.

Most of the papers are printed from a computer. I can't understand what they say any better than if they were written by hand. There are some words I recognize, words that are in prayer books. *Thanks*. And *help*. And *girls*. Buried in one paragraph I find the word *hell*. The words I know are sprinkled like morning dew on grass, tiny windows that don't help me understand the whole.

In a beige folder I find a stack of images. There are

women posing, most of them without shirts or bras.

Some of them without panties.

I know it's wrong to look at them—wrong to have them—but I linger anyway. I look at their eyes made dark with blue and purple and black glitter. I look at their lips painted every shade of red. I look at the hair between their legs, trimmed into a neat shape or missing completely. I've never even cut the hair on my head, much less the hair *there.* I didn't know that was possible.

I can't stop thinking about it.

Would it hurt? It seems like it must hurt. Then my hand is gently pressing against myself, right *there,* over my shift, protective and terrified and curious.

The scrape comes from the door again, and my hand snaps to my side. My face heats with shame that he would come back and catch me this way. I slam the folder shut, but some images slide out anyway.

The door swings open.

It isn't him. Disappointment rises in me, unwelcome and grim. Why would I look forward to seeing him? He might end up hurting me.

I remember the cold glint in his eye, the promise.

Oh, he'll definitely end up hurting me.

Instead it's the guard who had been standing outside the basement door when we came in. I'd barely gotten a glance at him, enough to know he was big and tall and strong. He's dressed in all black, which adds to my impression of him as some kind of soldier. The only break in the image is the steaming tray of food he's carrying.

He sets it on the desk and eyes the photographs peeking out from the folder.

The folder that I'm holding down with my palm flat, as if I can keep the strange feelings it inspires locked up tight, far away from me.

He raises his eyebrows. "I won't tell on you for snooping."

"If?" I may be new here, but I already know everything comes with a price. This isn't so different from Harmony Hills, under all the lights.

He grins, looking boyish despite the fact that he's obviously armed and dangerous. "If you eat your vegetables."

I glance down at the tray he's holding and see a feast. All that is meant for one person? I've never even seen a plate that large, and it's piled high with food. There's a steak with the juices still sizzling and mashed potatoes, the butter almost completely melted, and emerald-green broccoli. I haven't eaten since dinner in the Great Hall last night, and my stomach grumbles loudly.

He gestures to the tray. "Come on, eat. You look like you're about to fall over."

He's right, so I round the desk and head back for the plain wooden chair. No way I'm sitting in the big leather swivel chair. I'd probably get struck by lightning or something.

Except I can't exactly sit down yet. "Are you…going to stay and watch?"

He gets a funny look on his face, almost embarrassed. "Just until you finish. Then I'll take the tray back upstairs."

I cock my head. I'm curious about him, but he sets me at ease. Completely unlike Ivan. "Why?"

He shrugs. "I don't question orders."

Unease twists my empty stomach. That's how it was in Harmony Hills, even if we called them counsels instead of orders. "What's your name?"

"It's Luca. And don't worry. I'm not going to hurt you." His brown eyes soften. "Or touch you."

I believe him, and that is the only reason I can sit and take a bite. And oh, that bite. The juices are still warm on my tongue, the steak more tender and wonderful than anything I've ever tasted. I catch Luca looking at me— looking at my lips—and my eyes widen.

His cheeks tinge red, and he turns away. "Where did you come from anyway?" he asks quietly. "Not from around here."

"Far away." Maybe not that far in miles. A hundred dollars didn't last long, but I might as well be on the other side of the world for how different all this looks— and how lonely I feel. "Your boss," I say softly.

"What about him?" Reserved. Wary.

Afraid?

"He's kind of…" I stammer, because I barely have the words for what I need to ask. "Can I trust him?"

That earns me a soft laugh. "Trust? I'm not sure anyone can *know* him, much less trust him. But if you stay in Tanglewood, you'll hear the stories."

"What kind of stories?"

"The kind that get told around campfires. Horror stories."

"Those aren't real."

"He is." The corner of Luca's mouth turns up. "The money that he puts in my account is real enough."

I can do anything I want with you.

The things he would do to me would be real enough too.

✧　✧　✧

THE FIRST TIME I ever rode in a car, I was eight years old.

A woman with kind eyes came and took me away. Mama had a strange look on her face, like she was trying to be brave, so I tried to be brave too. Even though the building scared me. And the people scared me.

They put me in a room with no windows. A camera was set up in the corner, watching me. I looked anywhere but at the shiny black lens. A doll slouched against the bench on the floor. Her hair was red. Building blocks climbed each other in the corner, every color of the rainbow. Who could play at a time like this, away from their family?

My heart beat a little faster, just looking at them. These were toys that hadn't been made in Harmony Hills, that hadn't been sanctioned by Leader Allen. I knew how wrong it was, and that made me want to do it more. I fought with myself for what felt like hours until the woman with kind eyes came back in. She had another person with her, a man. He smiled at me but stood silently in the corner while the woman asked questions.

How do you like living in Harmony Hills?
Who watches you?
Does anyone touch you? Where?

I answered all the questions as best I could, so I could go home. *I like it in Harmony Hills. Mama watches me. No one touches me, not ever.*

They weren't lies, not really. Most of the time I liked my life, but I didn't have a choice. I knew the woman wasn't really offering me one. And Mama did watch me most of the time, except when she was praying with Leader Allen. It took a long time, because her soul was so dark. At least, that's what Leader Allen told me.

The woman asked me that question a lot of times, using words in different ways so I would understand. Giving me a hug or giving me a bath didn't count. The way Leader Allen put his hand on my head when he was testing my faith, that didn't count either.

That was the day I learned that there was another kind of touch that might happen to me.

The next time I ever rode in a car was a bus that took me from Harmony Hills to the farthest place I could go. A city called Tanglewood.

"Come," Ivan says, and I don't hesitate. There's nothing for me in the basement of his business. This is like the room from before, with no windows. No toys on the floor, but I understood them now for what they were. Distractions. A kind of test, like the files on his desk. And probably there was a camera somewhere in the room, watching me. Seeing if I passed.

I follow him up the stairs, my gaze trained on his shoes. They shine, even in the dim light, and they make a harsh sound with every step. My shoes are blackened and completely silent. I'm his shadow as he leads me out a back door into the night.

Luca follows us to the car and opens the door.

Both men watch me expectantly. When I don't move, Ivan cocks his head. "In."

In. Just that, a short command. Like I'm an animal to be put in her cage. "Where are you taking me?"

"Home," he says.

That's what the woman said too, when we left the room. She drove me back to Harmony Hills, and he isn't taking me there. He's taking me somewhere strange, somewhere new. It isn't *my* home. Even so, hearing the word soothes me.

Because right now I don't have anywhere to go.

I climb into the back of his car. From the outside it looks like a regular car, except maybe a little more shiny. A little more smooth. From the inside, it's completely different. Nothing like the gray bus I came here on, with its plastic bucket seats and cracked window. It's nothing like the car the woman with kind eyes drove either, where she buckled me into the back and gave me a juice box.

This car doesn't even have seat belts, just incredibly soft seats. It's like running my hands over a cloud, and I do it again and again until Ivan sits beside me and I force my hands to still. There are buttons built into the sides of the car and a little panel in front of us with a screen. And a dark glass wall separating the front and the back.

Luca climbs in behind the wheel, and then the car glides forward.

I'm quiet the rest of the trip. So is Ivan.

Maybe he's thinking about work. But I know he's thinking about me. I can feel his attention on me even though he faces the front. His profile looks stark and forbidding, shadows stretching over his face, not quite covering him. I try to shrink myself, to become invisible. I hold my body very still. It's something I have a lot of practice with, in prayer.

Forgive me, for I have sinned...

CHAPTER FIVE

WE REACH IVAN'S house too quickly. I'm not ready to face what will happen to me here. Not ready to face that I've ended up in this position, at another man's mercy. Wasn't I supposed to get free? Isn't that why Mama risked everything?

Except a hundred dollars in cash and a brochure from the bus company didn't get me very far.

Deep inside, where I don't usually let myself feel, something sharp and hot burns. Frustration. Anger? Mama would know how to survive in the city. She lived in one before she went to Harmony Hills. Why didn't she teach me what I would need to know?

Why didn't she tell me about men like Ivan?

It doesn't matter now, because Luca opens the car door. I have no choice but to step outside and look up, up at the never-ending glass and concrete. It doesn't look like a house. It looks like a sculpture.

It almost looks like a church.

"No calls tonight," Ivan says, and Luca nods, wordless.

Luca holds the car door open for Ivan and then myself. Lights are set in the wall, high up, so the whole room is bathed in a pale light when we first arrive. Ivan touches a switch, and they grow brighter.

"This way," he says, leaving me behind.

I almost run to catch up, afraid to be left in this cold land of silver and white. It's winter, but not made by nature. Made by man. I don't know why anyone would make something so cold, but maybe Ivan wanted to see his reflection. Maybe he wanted to freeze.

He stops before I can, and I bump into him, the front of my body flush against his hard, unyielding back. I gasp and jump away. "Sorry."

Beyond a raised eyebrow, he ignores that. "There are clothes in the dresser," he says, gesturing to an open door. "And toiletries in the bathroom. Don't—"

I stand there, waiting to hear what I can't do. *Don't think sinful thoughts. Don't talk back.*

Don't run away and take a bus to a strange city.

I'm used to being told what not to do, and for most of my life, I obeyed.

"Don't wander," he says finally. "It might not be safe."

Might not be safe from what?

"I won't," I say softly. I'm too tired to wander. Too lost to even try. There's nowhere else to go.

"Get ready for bed," he says.

His words ring in my head while I go into the room and shut the door. They ring while I find the clothes in the dresser, a random assortment of feminine things, soft T-shirts and dresses, different sizes and colors. Who do they belong to? They ring while I shower under the hot spray, water burning away the smell of the city.

Get ready for bed.

Almost as if I'm to wait for him. As if he'll be joining me.

The bed is the largest one I've ever seen, but somehow too small for two people. Too small if one of the people is Ivan. He's physically large and, more than that, terrifying. What will he do to me? I can't fight him. God, I'm not sure I want to try. *Home.*

In the end I push back the heavy blankets, almost as thick as my sleeping pallet in Harmony Hills, and climb onto the bed. The pillow is perfectly soft, so clean, and I let myself drift away. I'm floating on a cloud, plush and high up.

I dream in those moments. I dream about color and light. I dream about the sky.

There is a deep voice from above and all around me, telling me to get on my knees. Commanding me to pray. This is the first time in my life I've ever skipped bedtime prayers. The first time I haven't begged for salvation. I'm not going to beg, not ever again.

The hand on my face doesn't feel angry. It isn't a slap for my insolence. It strokes down my temple and cups my cheek. My eyes flutter open. *Ivan.*

His hand falls away.

"Candace," he says in the same deep voice of my dream.

And there's a look in his eyes, the same look Leader

Allen gives Mama. The same look he started giving me. That look is the reason Mama sent me away.

"You'll stay here," he says softly. "I don't want you to dance, but you can stay."

The allure of it beats through me, a heart of its own, thumping away to a dream that isn't mine. Safety. *Home.* I want those things, but I want freedom more. I want the flash of lights and of skin. I want the power those women had onstage.

Ivan wants to put me in a cage, but what I really want is to fly.

"Okay," I lie, because one sin becomes many. Leader Allen taught me that, and he was right. I'll convince Ivan, though. One day I'll dance on that stage, and Ivan will watch me.

One day he'll teach me everything there is to know.

"Good girl."

The praise washes over me, undeserved and darkly pleasurable, a stroke along my spine. It feels good, but I know what it is. A trap. A chain around my ankle to keep me on the ground. In this moment, it locks me so tight that I'd accept anything he did to me. If he were to *touch* me the way the woman with the kind eyes meant. The way Leader Allen touches Mama during prayer.

Ivan leans down, and I hold my breath. Large hands take hold of the blanket, lift slightly. I feel everything between us—anticipation and denial, lust and fear corded together. We feel them together, breathe them in through the air, pulse them with each beat of our hearts.

It's a kind of knowledge, this feeling, connecting a thousand nerve points to the core of my body. This is what he meant by teaching me. This and so much more.

Then he pulls the blanket higher, tucking it around me. "Good night," he says, eyes glittering in the dark.

He is silver and light, made even brighter by the shadows behind him. It's strange, the disappointment I feel that he isn't going to touch me. He isn't going to *teach* me. Not tonight. "Good night," I whisper back.

Then he's gone, shutting the door against the dark, locking me in. And I slide away into sleep, without dreams, without color, with only the shameless black of contentedness, knowing I am safe for the night.

CHAPTER SIX

Three years later

WALKING THROUGH THE Grand is like walking through a dream. A sweet dream, most nights. Flashing lights and bright colors. And sex. It coats these dreams with honey, thick and burnished gold.

There are bad dreams too, on nights when a new asshole walks through the doors and puts his hand on me. Security is quick to throw them out, when they see, and Ivan swift and merciless with retribution, when he finds out. And for those few minutes when nobody knows, when I'm alone with some new monster…well, everyone gets nightmares sometimes.

"You going onstage?" Bianca asks. She's relatively new to the club, an ice queen, her gait more of a glide. She surveys me from a few inches higher, her plastic glass slippers raising her above me.

Of course I know her aloofness is an act. She's actually a scaredy cat when it comes to Ivan, or most men actually, which is why she's here.

"I'm done for the night," I tell her. "Heading back now."

"Oh." She examines her nails, a shimmery opal. "Do

you think you could check about that time off?"

"And the reason you can't ask him yourself is because…" We put our schedules together at the beginning of every two weeks. Now she needs tomorrow off for some unspecified reason.

The mask cracks, just for a moment. "I need this. I *really* need this time off, and he's more likely to say yes to you. Please. It's…personal."

She says *personal* like it's a dirty word, and in here, it is. We don't pass around a sharing stick in the dressing room. This isn't a goddamn therapy session. No, we bury our issues deep, where it can turn our souls black, numb us from the inside out, like any other self-respecting stripper.

"I'll talk to him," I say, because it seems like the fastest way to make her stop.

"Thank you," she says, relief evident. "I'll owe you one."

"Yeah, yeah," I mutter, stalking past her. I hadn't planned on talking to Ivan tonight. He will definitely notice my shaky hands. And with his bruisers reporting my every move, he'll know why.

The crowd is decent tonight, a teeming mass I have to fight my way through, pushing and shoving just to stay upright. I get off on this—the noise, the people. The looks men give me as I pass them by. It's why I loved this place the moment I stumbled into the club, wide-eyed and terrified. It's why I begged and pleaded to be allowed onstage, back before I was quite legal—the lone nameless, underage girl in his otherwise legitimate enterprise.

And it's why I put up with what happens in the basement. Not sex. God, nothing as pedestrian as that. Ivan could get sex from any of the girls in Tanglewood. For all I know, he does. It's something different he wants from me, though.

Luca stands watch at the stairwell, face impassive. "Evening," he says.

I smile, enjoying the challenge. I've gotten to know Luca Almanzar pretty well since we first met. And he can be pretty fun, except when he's on duty. He's like one of those guards outside the palace, a tall hat and an unbreakable stare.

Pressing myself close, I run my hand down his chest. I'm an inch away from him when I whisper, "Good evening to you too, handsome."

He stiffens at my touch, at my words, but he doesn't break formation. "Do you want to get me killed?"

"Buzzkill," I say, leaning back.

One dark eyebrow rises. "I want to live," he says drily.

It makes me laugh, and I poke him in his rock-hard abs. Of course it does nothing. He's like a damn statue. "You've gotten more serious since I met you."

"And you've gotten less."

I freeze. Direct hit. "Is that so bad?"

He sighs. "No, it's good. I'm glad you're happy, Candy. *If* you're happy."

What the hell was happiness anyway? An orgasm? A

pill? I'd mapped out almost every pleasure known to man and still hadn't quite found mine. Years of dancing, of drinking. Years of being watched by Ivan, wondering if he'd pounce. The only thing I knew for sure was that I couldn't keep going like this.

"I need to talk to him," I murmur. An afterthought, even though Ivan is anything but.

He's my first thought when I wake from a bender. My last before I take a hit.

"He's in a mood," Luca says.

When is he not? I don't bother asking. Luca wouldn't have an answer. No, I make my way down the stairs. I'll just have to hide my trembling hands and shaky legs. I'll have to hide how dry my mouth feels.

Hide how badly I want a drink.

It's been three years since I first walked down these steps. I spent the first year locked up in his house, barely touched, barely noticed, left with books and music and dancing all alone. I finally convinced Ivan to let me dance in the Grand. He even got me my own apartment. But through it all, Ivan has always been there—directing my movements, picking my clothes, watching me. Waiting for me to make a mistake so that he can punish me.

I can't keep going this way. Not even for Ivan.

CHAPTER SEVEN

I T'S COLD IN the basement, without the body heat and the spotlights. Cold and damp. I wonder how Ivan's desk can survive the moisture in the air, how it doesn't rot, but the old carved wood continues to stand, incongruous and proud.

Ivan doesn't look up when I step into the room. He knows Luca would guard that damn door with his life— or at least knock and announce the visitor if it's club business.

Except for me.

I can come down here whenever I want. That's the only thing that's up to me. Because as soon as that metal door clangs shut behind me, I'm sealed in. Ivan's in charge of me now.

And he wants me to wait.

There's a feeling that comes over me while I stand there, in the middle of a cold, dark room. The same feeling I had on my knees for hours, reciting my prayers under the watchful eyes of Leader Allen. I was a child then, even if he didn't always see me that way.

I'm not a child now...

Even if Ivan continues to treat me like one.

"Come," he says finally, pen still to paper. He makes a final stroke, almost violent—his signature.

I cross the floor. The spikes of my heels barely touch the ground. It used to sound impossibly loud, the clack of shoes. And though I embraced so many loud and bright and immoral things about my new life, that was one I couldn't shake. So I learned to walk quietly in my heels.

I stand directly in front of his desk, the tops of my thighs inches away from the edge. "Bianca wants to know if she can have tomorrow off."

Pale gray eyes meet mine. "And the reason she isn't asking me herself is?"

"Because you're intimidating and, let's face it, a cold motherfucker. She's scared of you."

That earns me something—a suggestion of a smile, a tilt of his lips. "But you're not."

"Should I be?" I challenge, but I already know the answer is yes. I'm scared, but I'm here anyway. What does that say about me? "I can cover for Bianca tomor-row."

"Can you?" he says, which is his way of saying *yes*. His gaze sweeps over me like a tangible touch, taking in my ruffled lace bra-and-panties set in a pale, peachy pink. My nipples harden under his hot gaze, even through the gauzy fabric. "You work too much already."

I give him a saucy smile, the same way I'd do for a customer. "I still find plenty of time to play."

His lids lower. "Play," he repeats, tasting the word.

Oh shit. There's doubt in that one word. And derision. And unarguable dominance. It drops my chin to my chest and my eyes to the floor. I'm no longer the sassy, sarcastic stripper who flirted with Luca upstairs. Now I'm standing under Ivan's scrutiny, waiting for him to pass judgment.

"And have you been good?" he asks.

"Yes," I say.

But with just that one word, I prove myself wrong. He frowns at me. That frown. That stern expression, the forbidding glint in his eyes. I dream of his face this way, of all it means, of what comes next. *This is a dream.*

"Yes, sir." It's not what he wants to be called, not exactly.

He gives me a short nod. "You ate?"

On Harmony Hills there were acres of wheat, of corn. And the table—the table was empty. We were fed according to how much we had sinned. When I misbehave, I have a tendency to punish myself. Ivan doesn't like this.

He's the only one who can punish me now.

"Enough," I say.

"You slept well?"

God, this concern. So twisted and fake and perfect. It slices through me, right to the core of regret and longing. I shrug.

One eyebrow rises. "Or did you go out last night?"

He knows I didn't. The men watching me would have told him I didn't leave my apartment. When I first came to Ivan, he got me tutors and textbooks. I started at a third-grade level and worked my way to high school level in the year that I lived with him. Meanwhile he dressed me up and sheltered me. And I knew I would never really grow up unless I left. So I demanded to move out, insisted on dancing at the Grand, and he allowed it as long as he could monitor my every move.

I'm a different person now. No one could recognize me, my hair like silk instead of straw, my skin flushed and tanned and powered instead of flat. I've filled out too. Good food has given me curves instead of a stick-thin body.

As much as I've changed, I can't leave my past behind.

Someone won't let me leave my past behind.

"I didn't go out." The truth sucks the air from the room. Even in his presence, I can feel another one. "I was too afraid, after…"

After someone broke into the Grand. After someone left a note scrawled across my vanity mirror with my pink-bubblegum lipstick. *John 10:16.* A Bible verse. Of course I recognized what it was. And of course I remembered what it said. The lessons are too ingrained in me to ever forget, imprinted on my mind and in my skin. Ivan was convinced it was a random attack, just another creep in the clientele, but I knew otherwise.

And I have other sheep that are not of this fold. I must bring them also, and they will listen to my voice. So there will be one flock, one shepherd.

I may take off my clothes on that stage, but it's not me they're seeing. Glitter and flash. Artifice. Inside I'm still a follower. Ivan's always seen that in me.

"Come here," he says, no tenderness in his voice. There's pure fury.

He likes me afraid, as long as he's the one making me that way.

Ivan has increased security at the Grand in recent months. He's increased security on me too. He's always had me followed, always known when I did something worth punishing. Before, I'd feel their eyes watching me from the shadows, a constant presence. Now they stand in plain sight, actual bodyguards—not the least bit subtle.

I circle the desk to stand in front of him. A beat starts up in my body, the thrum of my heart made faster, louder, pulsing right between my legs. I'm trapped in this game like I'm trapped in this basement. The ropes are made from my own lust, with his strong hands tying the knots.

"You don't think about that," Ivan says sternly, but what I hear is, *You don't think about him.* He's talking about the man who left the note. I'm thinking about the man I left behind. "He won't touch you. No one will ever fucking touch you."

I want freedom. I want to feel safe. Those two things are opposite desires, and they tear me apart. He turns me on. He conditions me for this. But it's not either of those things that keep me here. It's hope, that one day he'll somehow do both of those things for me—he'll set me free and catch me when I fall.

"Except you." A challenge and a plea at once.

He leans back, his expression dark. For just a second I see desire. I see longing. He wants more than what we have in this basement, this dungeon—more than the scraps he gives himself. Then the emotion is wiped away as if it was never there. His face is impassive. He's a statue, as cold and unyielding as the concrete walls around us.

His head tilts toward the desk. "Bend over."

My heart beats faster. I don't want to bend over the desk. I want to be over his lap, to feel him getting hard underneath me. I want to be held by him, touched by him, surrounded by him.

"Candace," he says, using my real name—and it works. It snaps me right into place, that headspace where all I can do is obey.

The desk is cool against my front, pressing against my breasts, the closest he comes to a caress. I push down my ruffled panties until they're around my thighs, trapping me in place. Exposing me to his gaze and to his rage.

Then he's standing behind me. "Did you drink last night?" he asks conversationally.

I remember staring at the bottle, half-full of amber liquid. I remember the dryness of my mouth, the knot in my throat. I didn't want it. But I wanted this. "Yes," I whisper.

Only a sip. A sip is all it takes.

His hand comes at me swiftly, a whoosh of air one second before impact. My whole body jerks. Pain explodes in my butt and spreads over my skin like wildfire.

"Well?" he asks, one hand fisting in my hair. He lifts, and I stare into the dark, empty hole that is my life. This basement, this man. This need we both share, under cover of night.

My voice is wobbly. My whole body is wobbly. "Thank you, sir."

His fist gives me a little shake before he lets me go. I rest my cheek on the desk.

Another blow, this one even harder. There are no warmups, no mercy. Only punishment.

The slightest sound escapes me, a moan, a whimper. "Thank you, sir."

He leans over me, careful not to touch. Only the faintest ghost of a feeling, his suit fabric against my naked skin. "Did you shoot up?" he asks.

"No," I tell him, feeling the tears rise in my throat. I couldn't bring myself to do it, didn't want the rush. Didn't want the pain.

That gives him pause. I feel his hesitation hover around us. "Did you smoke?"

"No."

He stands, cool air replacing his body heat. "Were you a good girl, Candace?"

I can't hold the sob in. It comes out of me, wrenching my body, relief and regret in one pained sound. "No, sir. No. I wasn't. I—I touched myself."

His satisfaction wraps around me like velvet, dark and seductive. Of course he wants more though. Whatever I give him, he always wants more. "Where did you touch yourself?"

I shudder. "No, don't...don't make me tell you."

His hand rests on the curve of my ass, his thumb brushing over my heated flesh, back and forth. He hurts me and he soothes me, but never enough. Back and forth. Never enough pain or pleasure. He always leaves me needing more.

Back and forth. "No, little one. You're going to show me."

There are vines that wrap around me, their thorns pressing in, making me bleed. Being with Ivan doesn't free me from the vines. He doesn't make the pain go away. He makes me want more.

I shove my hand down, graceless, unpracticed, under my body and between my legs. I don't slide my hand under my panties or finger my clit, not the way I did last night. I just cup myself, protective, afraid.

"What did you do next?" His voice is low, the grate of stone on stone. "Daddy needs to see."

My eyes squeeze tight, and I shake my head. *I can't.* I sin again and again, over and over. And every time, in the seconds before, with my very last breath, I'm fighting it. Fighting myself. Fighting *him.*

"Show me," he coaxes, his voice dark and hypnotic. I

would follow that voice anywhere. Even into hell.

I press one finger inside my pussy, where I'm already wet, where I'm burning up with lust and shame. I know my cheeks are pink even though my eyes are closed. They'll match my bubblegum lipstick.

"That's right," he says with a sigh. "Can you find your little clit? I'm sure it's nice and hard."

My fingers slide through my wetness and settle on my clit. It's a hard nub, throbbing at the faint friction. "It is. *Please.*"

"Good little girls aren't supposed to touch themselves, are they?"

I'm not a little girl. The words are on the tip of my tongue, but I don't say them. I can't. I can't add a lie to my sin. Because I am a little girl. I'm Ivan's little girl, for as long as he'll have me. Even if this is all I'll ever be to him.

"I'm not good," I say instead.

"I know. And I'm going to punish you. You'll touch your clit while I spank you, and then you'll learn what happens to bad girls."

I don't hear the next blow coming. It takes me by surprise, and I jerk, pressing my clit into my hand. Pleasure arcs through me, white-hot from my breasts against the desk to my toes curled on the floor. I moan and rock my hips, seeking more of the pleasure to take away the pain. The next blow comes too fast, and then he's hitting me in earnest, beating me—it's too much. My fingers on my clit only make me sensitized, only make me more aware of every ounce of pain.

I can almost feel the calluses on his palm, the signs that he once fought in the streets before he came to rule them. I imagine I can feel the lines of his fingerprints, uniquely him, branding me for his own. It's at once a sharp blade and a wide blast, cutting me to pieces and spreading me apart.

He hits me harder and faster, until I can feel each blow reverberate inside me. The pain isn't outside me anymore; it's inside, digging deep. I can't reach this any other way. Not with alcohol, not with dancing. And sure as hell not with sex. Only this—being hit over and over again by a man who cares enough to do it. He doesn't love me, not the way a man does a woman. He takes care of me. He disciplines me.

He draws a circle around me and then hurts me when I step outside it.

It's the reason I've stepped outside the line so damn much. *This.*

"I can't," I whisper, voice broken. I'm sobbing now. This is what he's reduced me to. A crying little girl, a mess. I'm clinging to the desk. *I wish I was over his lap.*

I'd be able to feel his erection pressing into my belly. I'd be able to rub against it.

"Can't what?" he asks, only faintly curious. He isn't even breathing hard.

"Can't do it anymore," I manage between sobs.

I think he knows what's coming. That's why he rains down blows on my already aching ass. Much more and

I'll have bruises tomorrow. I won't be able to go onstage, but then maybe that's the point. He's never wanted me to dance.

He hits me until I'm crying even harder, until I'm begging him to stop. *No, please, it's too much, it's too hard, please stop, I'll be good, I'll be good, I'll be good.*

Then he does stop. "What?"

"I'll be good," I say again, the words too garbled to understand. He understands anyway.

When he speaks, his voice is deeper, breath coming faster. He could beat me all day, but this is what he wants. This gentleness, this surrender. He has to break me down to get it.

God, he'd be so hard right now.

"I'll be good, Daddy. I'm so sorry. I'll be your good girl now." The words keep pouring out of me, promises and pleas. And prayers.

That's what he is to me, a new Leader Allen. My personal god.

Ivan replaced everything that came before. I could leave Harmony Hills, but I couldn't change who I was. I still needed to worship. I still need to obey.

"Shh," he tells me. "That's right. You're my good girl."

I slide off the desk, my ass still burning from the sting of his palm. The floor is unyielding against my knees, but I don't care. I cling to his pant leg, feeling him through the wool. I press my face against his thigh, turning the fabric damp. "Please. Let me serve you. Let me, let me…"

"Shh," he says again, brushing the hair back from my forehead. "Enough of that. You're forgiven."

He's absolved me, but that isn't enough. I need him to touch me, to feel what I see bulging his suit pants. I need to be more than a servant or a thing to save. *I need to be a woman.*

Is this how my mother felt?

I never understood why she went to Harmony Hills, why she let Leader Allen use her like a whore. Wasn't it a sin? He punished her every day. Only now do I understand, when I crave the same thing from a man far less holy and a lot more dangerous.

Ivan's thumb brushes my tears from my cheeks. "Don't cry, little one."

And then I can't hold back the truth. I have to tell him what I couldn't say before. This can't go on. I want him to hurt me, to discipline me. I want him to *touch* me, even if that will only ever happen in the form of his palm on my ass. But I can't go on like this. I can't keep drinking and partying. I'm not even sure I can keep dancing. "I can't keep being bad," I whisper, looking up into his gray eyes. "I have to be good now."

If I'm good, he can't bend me over the desk anymore. He can't punish me.

This would never happen. Regret flickers in his eyes. It's immediately replaced by the cold detachment that all the other girls get. This is why they're scared to talk to him. This is who they see.

"I don't believe you," he says, as dark as the shadows around us. "Now go, little one. Run away."

CHAPTER EIGHT

I DO LEAVE, but I come back again the next night. This is our dance, this attack and retreat—with one exception. Each time I left, I would do something wrong. Something so he would touch me.

Something so he would punish me.

When I show up at the Grand in late afternoon, shadows stretch over the cobblestone. The sun has left a sticky sweetness in the air, not quite evaporated by the night's chill. I haven't taken a sip of alcohol or a hit of anything. I haven't even given myself an orgasm. I haven't done a single thing to take the edge off, so I'm wired. I blink against blinding sideways light, feeling every bead of sweat on my skin. The world is too sharp like this, the very air made of blades.

I'm panting by the time I make it inside the double doors. They swing shut behind me, blocking out most of the light. I suck in the stale air like it's a lifeline.

West is sitting at the bar. He works security here, one of the bouncers. Luckily he's too busy brooding into his glass to notice me practically panting from panic. His dark skin looks even darker under the bar's tinny overhead lights.

"Drinking on the job?" I ask, leaning against the bar. "I didn't know a Boy Scout like you had it in you."

He looks up, expression wry. "It's water."

I hop onto the stool next to him and peer into the glass he's been staring at. "Water is never that interesting. There something bothering you?"

"Are you going to tell Ivan if there is?" His voice is mild, almost teasing, but I detect the warning there as well. I'm an outsider, even here, in this place. The girls look up to me just as much as they look down on me. They want my help, but they hold me at arm's length. That's what I get for fucking the boss.

Or *not* fucking the boss, in our twisted little game.

"Well, I don't think you're stealing the silver. So no, I don't think I'd have to run and tattle on you."

Besides, in a very short amount of time, it won't even matter. I won't be here anymore, and I doubt Ivan will even want to see me again.

"Not stealing the silver, no. But…" He grimaces. "Looking at it."

"And the silver in this case being…girls."

"Shit. I'm sorry. I didn't mean it like that."

He looks miserable, and I have to laugh. It's not every day I meet a man who even cares that he might have offended me, much less one who avoids objectifying us. "Don't worry about it. I mean, looking is free. And kind of a job requirement for you, since if you didn't look at us, you couldn't protect us. So I'm guessing you mean one girl in particular."

"On my first day here I met with Ivan. He told me don't fuck—" He clears his throat. "Don't mess with the girls. I didn't think it would be a problem for me. Hell, it *shouldn't* be a problem for me."

"This is one Ivan problem I can't help you with. You want a day off or a free hour in the VIP room? Come talk to me. This is one area where Ivan can't be moved."

"Then why—" West stops speaking abruptly, and I have a feeling he's blushing, even though it's too dark to see. He stands, unfolding to his six-foot height. He towers over me, but he's sheepish. Worried he disrespected me. With another man, I'd think he didn't want to offend Ivan. In this case West doesn't want to offend *me.* He's that kind of guy, old-world manners. He fits in well with the Grand, with the crumbling building and its faded damask wallpaper. Even if it is a strip club.

"Why does he fuck me?" I fill in for him. "He doesn't. That's the short answer."

West blinks in surprise. I know what everyone thinks. And with what Ivan does to me in that basement, they're not completely wrong. He hurts me and uses me in depraved ways. But he doesn't fuck me. He doesn't even touch my pussy. I've never seen his cock.

"It's none of my business," West says softly. "You don't have to explain yourself. Or him."

"Good thing, because I wouldn't know what to tell you. But don't let Ivan catch you fucking around with one of the girls. He's protective of them."

He gives me a faint smile. "That's one of the reasons

I like working here. And why I'd like to keep working here."

I tell myself it's concern for the girls that has me asking and not prurient curiosity, but that's a lie. It's both. "So who is the lucky girl?"

"Lucky isn't the word I'd use to describe her," West says darkly.

And I know exactly what he means even if that doesn't clear it up any. Every girl here has a story. No one grew up wanting to take their clothes off for men. Even if the ideal sounds sexy, the reality doesn't live up to it. Panting men and grasping hands. Lots of money, but never enough to feel clean.

That's what I didn't know when I wanted to work here. I feel powerful onstage, flaunting my nakedness, using my sexuality to lead men around. But at the end of the day the power is only an illusion.

West takes a long drink from his glass of water, emptying it. "Anyway, I'm not trying to mess around with her. It's not like that. I just want to…"

He trails off, but I know the answer. Ironically it's the same thing Ivan wanted when he saw me. It's the reason we're trapped in this perverted standoff, spanking and mouthing off, ever circling. "You want to save her," I say sadly. "But that's the thing about girls. We can only save ourselves."

CHAPTER NINE

RUFFLES AND LACE are my armor. Lipstick and glitter, my war paint. Going to the basement without any of it makes me feel vulnerable. I'm wearing a baby-blue tank top and a low-riding pair of jeans, but I may as well be in a dirty white shift.

I told West that girls have to save themselves, and that's what I'm doing. It won't feel powerful, like I do when I'm onstage, in my armor and war paint, but it will be real.

All I can do is nod to Luca on the way down.

Ivan doesn't look up when I reach the bottom. He knows it's me, but I have to wait. And I'll give him this much, one last time.

"Come," he says finally, and I step forward.

Surprise flickers in his pale eyes only briefly. Then it's gone. He doesn't even wait for me to speak, like he usually does. He doesn't ask why I'm here, hours earlier than I usually arrive. "Have you been a good girl?" he asks.

Maybe I should take comfort in that. He wants what we have, however dark and deviant, enough to try to keep it. He must sense something is changing, and he wants it to stay the same.

I can't go back, though. The thing that's changing is me. I came here as a scared, lost little girl. I rose out of those ashes and became someone beautiful, someone powerful. Someone who never really existed. I'll leave this room the same way I came—scared and lost. A little girl, even if I'm no longer his.

"Yes," I say softly. I'm good and I'm alone. Those are the same things. Aren't they?

He stands, sudden and almost aggressive. He doesn't move around the desk. He just narrows his eyes. "Why did you come, Candace? What do you need?"

I need so much more than he'll give me. Touch, acceptance. Love. "I quit."

Molten silver. That's what fury looks like, streaking across his eyes. "Excuse me?"

"I quit."

His laugh cuts me inside. "What do you want? More money? More pain? Should I start using a cane on you?"

Is this all I needed to do, threaten to leave? It's too late for that. Maybe those things would have been enough. They might have kept me here for a few more months, at least. I'm dangling off a cliff, and I'll keep scrabbling at loose rocks on the way down. That's all he can offer me: loose rocks. I know it's going to hurt at the bottom—God, it will hurt. But I can't keep grasping for him. I have to fall.

"I'm sorry," I tell him.

That was a mistake. He stalks around the desk, and I

tense. I'm not afraid that he'll hurt me. Not exactly. He'll find something much worse than that. A way to punish me for leaving. I think what would hurt the worst is if he said nothing at all. If he could watch me go, just as casually as I'm acting, as if it's not tearing him down inside.

"No," he says, so softly it's barely a sound.

I should have expected this. Not punishment. Denial. "I know you're upset with me, but I've made up my mind."

"Have you?" he asks, his voice strangely pleasant. "And what makes you think it's up to you?"

My heart beats faster. "What do you mean?"

His smile is a baring of teeth. A threat. A promise. "You understand me, little one. You always have. What the fuck makes you think I'm going to let you walk up those stairs?"

Fight-or-flight. That's my first reaction to his words. I want to run up those stairs, fast enough that he can't catch me. I want to lash out at him for making me feel afraid. "What are you going to do, keep me chained up in a basement?" I laugh unsteadily. "Even if you don't care that it's illegal, it seems a little cliché for you."

Bad move.

Three seconds later I'm slammed up against the wall, Ivan's forearm at my throat, his face an inch away from mine. "You think I give a fuck about clichés? Or the fucking law? Do you?"

I can't breathe, and the fear I've been pushing back

claws its way up my throat. "Please."

"You think you can just walk away, like these years mean nothing?"

They do mean nothing, because he's never going to make it real.

I didn't want to feel anything. I didn't want to *let* myself feel anything. I was content to drink and smoke and rub my clit into oblivion. The ice has been cracking now, for months. Even when I walked down those steps, there was part of it still intact.

It cracks now, an actual shattering sensation in my chest.

"Ivan," I whisper, and a tear tracks down my cheek.

He watches it fall. "Am I hurting you that much?"

Not with his arm against my throat. Not with his body holding mine. But he is hurting me. He's breaking me into pieces. "I wanted us to be real. I want for you to—" *For you to love me.* "I tried so many times, and I just....I can't. Not anymore."

"Real," he scoffs. "What the fuck is real?"

"I don't know." And that's the honest-to-God truth. I don't know what a real relationship is like. I don't think he does either. "But I know it's not this."

He presses even harder, and black spots dance in front of my eyes. He's really going to do it. My brain is going soft and foggy, the edges drawing in, but that's the thought that stands out—a kind of gentle amazement that he's really going to do it. Make me black out. Maybe even kill me.

I stare into his eyes. I'm not even fighting him. However this ends, it will be over.

My lungs burn from the lack of oxygen, my whole body folding in on itself. The world seems light, insubstantial. I'm floating…

A loud *crack* jerks me from my reverie. Ivan pulls back in surprise, and my body sucks in a breath all on its own, bringing me back to life and making me choke. Footsteps ring out on the metal steps, fast and heavy.

Luca appears at the entrance, his expression grim. There's an unholy light in his eyes, violence and blood reflected back. He doesn't seem surprised to find me in a choke hold. "You'd better come upstairs," he says. "Both of you."

LUCA'S TIMING IS so lucky I might have thought he'd done it on purpose to save me. But I know the truth. The basement is truly soundproof. Ivan could keep me down here for the rest of my life—and no one would hear my screams. And besides, Luca would never go against Ivan. Not even for me.

Ivan studies his bodyguard for a moment. Then his gaze slides to me. I can see him deliberating whether he wants to let me go to the surface. Whether he thinks I'll make a run for it.

"Sir," Luca says, and I hear something in that voice. Something I've never heard from the street-hardened man—a sliver of fear.

Ivan must hear it too. "Show me."

He doesn't exactly let me go upstairs. Nothing as gentlemanly as allowing me to walk ahead of him. No, he heads upstairs. And I'm free to follow, even though I'm still shuddering. The air feels like glass, and I'm sucking it in by the lungful. My body doesn't believe that I'll be able to take another breath, so it's hoarding them, making me pant even when I've had enough.

We reach the top, and the hallway is empty. That's not that strange considering how early it is, but my skin pricks. The hair on the back of my neck rises, and I don't think it's only because of Luca's strange behavior. There's something in the air, a metal tang. *Blood.*

That's the first thing I see when we push into the alleyway. Buckets of blood. A goddamn river of it, coating the ground and mingling in the ever-present puddles. Some of it's clotted. I clap my hand over my mouth, smothering my cry and keeping myself from throwing up. I want to cry. I want to scream. But all I can do is stand there, frozen.

"Where's the body?" Ivan asks, his voice cold. He sounds almost unaffected. God, maybe he *is* unaffected. What's a little blood to clean up? Or a lot of blood…

I don't know how he even noticed there wasn't a body, but now that I look—there isn't one. Only blood. It's actually creepier this way, without a source.

"We're pulling the tapes," Luca says. "We'll find out what happened."

West is there, looking serious.

So is Oscar, the head of security. "I already called Blue," he says. "And the cops."

Ivan's face is a stone mask. "We'll handle this in-house. Heads will roll."

Heads will roll. Violence and more violence. Blood and more blood. A hysterical laugh bubbles out of me. Only then do they look over at me.

West seems concerned, Oscar angry.

Luca seems disgusted.

And Ivan…he seems like he always does. Calm. Calculating.

"Get back inside," he says, somehow cool in the face of this gore.

I'm rooted to the spot, unnaturally drawn to the gruesome scene, straight out of my nightmares. The Grand has always been my safe place. And now that I've decided to leave, the dreams have found me here.

"Inside," he repeats.

"I'm done listening to you," I say, and even I can hear the panic in my voice, the high-pitched thread of fear. "You don't get to order me around. You don't even get to *talk* to me."

Ivan stares at me, and I imagine him slapping me. I imagine him pushing me against the bloodstained brick and choking the life out of me. I imagine him turning me over the trash can and spanking me.

His expression softens. "It's okay, Candy. Look at me. Focus on me. You're okay."

"I'm not." My voice is shaky. It's my little-girl voice,

the one I only use for him. Except now West and Oscar and Luca are hearing it too. Not just as part of an act, with a dress-up schoolgirl outfit and pigtails. This is the real little girl that's buried inside me, right on the surface.

Ivan sees it too. He reacts to it, even if he doesn't want to. "I want you to go inside and wait for me. Right now."

"I'm scared," I whisper. "It's happening again."

A month ago there was a message left on my vanity mirror with bubblegum lipstick. John 10:16. A Bible verse. A warning. And now this, a river of blood. Ivan believed that was a random attack, but it felt familiar. And this feels personal.

Ivan doesn't deny it. "I'm going to fix this," he says, right there in the back alley, in front of Luca and West, with the seedy downtown Tanglewood as my witness. "Daddy will make it right."

He holds me tight, and only when I'm wrapped in his arms, turned sideways, do I see it.

Scrawled across the crumbling brick of the Grand is a message. No bubblegum lipstick this time. This one is written in blood. *Peter 2:25.*

CHAPTER TEN

I MEANT TO leave the Grand tonight, to quit, to go somewhere else and start over again, just like I did years ago. It broke my heart to even think about it. Leaving the Grand and the girls. Leaving my friends, especially Honey and Lola. And Clara, though I really should never have befriended her.

And most of all, leaving Ivan. It broke my heart more than I'd been willing to admit, and there was a part of me that had wanted him to make good on his threat to keep me down in that basement. If I didn't have a choice, it wouldn't be my fault. It wouldn't be my sin.

But after all that hoping, all that heartbreak, here I am in Ivan's house, tucked into my old room.

Right where I started.

I close my eyes again. I don't even remember how I ended up in this bed. Did I walk here? Did he carry me? The walls are bare, painted a pale cream. No windows. The sheets are white and soft as butter. The room is an expensive blank slate. An upgrade from my colorless days at Harmony Hills, but not much better.

My muscles are stiff when I pull myself out of bed. I'm wearing my baby blue tank top and peach-colored panties. My jeans are slung over a chair in the corner. It's dark outside, which means I must have slept for hours. I pause at the staircase and look out at the courtyard, more concrete than grass, walled in by a high brick fence. The front door opens directly to the street, the front of the house an impenetrable brick face. Around the back is a tall brick gate that surrounds a concrete courtyard. From up here, I can see the spikes in the top of the wall that keep someone from climbing over.

A few plants cling to life in ceramic pots around the space.

If there's one upside to being here, it's that I feel safe. Safe from whoever left those notes, if not entirely safe from Ivan. His house is more of a fortress than a home. I'm surprised there's not a moat surrounding us.

But then I guess the barbed wire and armed guards do the trick.

The lights are off downstairs, a deep stillness creating a kind of intimacy. I can feel Ivan's presence down here, a beating heart in one of the cold rooms. I search until I find him—his silhouette, seated at the head of the long, ornate dining table. I can see that he's wearing a suit. I'm guessing he never changed from earlier.

He's reclined in the high-backed chair, one leg slung over the other. It's a relaxed pose, but I can feel the tension running through his body. I can feel his eyes on me too.

He doesn't speak. Neither do I.

There's a book spread open on the gleaming table in

front of him. I don't even need to look closely to know it's a Bible. I have seen enough of them to recognize the thickness. I can almost smell the thin, ink-drenched pages. Where did Ivan get this? I can't help but wonder if he asked Luca to bring one to him. It almost makes me smile to think of him buying one—or stealing it.

I drop my finger to the words, barely making out the heading *Peter*. It's too dark in the room to see the letters. Has he been sitting here since the sun set?

I don't have to read to know what it says.

"'For ye were as sheep going astray; but are now returned unto the Shepherd and Bishop of your souls.'" Even soft, even hesitant, my voice rings out in the quiet.

"Did you sleep well?" he asks, solicitous.

"I should go," I say. "I already quit, and this…this doesn't change anything."

"Are you hungry? I had Rosa put a plate together. I'll heat it up for you."

Frustration rises in my chest. He'll take such good care of me, making sure I'm well fed and well slept. And well spanked, probably. He won't take care of what I need most. "Stop ignoring me, Ivan."

"You should go back to sleep. That wasn't enough for the night."

I stomp my foot. "Stop. Ignoring. Me."

His fist hits the table so fast and so hard I jump. "I'm not ignoring you, Candace." He leans forward, breathing hard. "You're all I can fucking think about every second of every fucking day. I have to know what you're doing,

61

where you are. I haven't treated you right, and the worst part is, I don't think I'm capable of it, but if there's one thing I've never done, it's ignore you."

I take in a shuddering breath. "God."

He flips the Bible shut with a bang. "Fuck this asshole who thinks he can fuck with my club. He's nothing. I'm going to find him and snuff him out like a fucking cigarette. You don't worry about him."

He's talking about the nameless, faceless stranger who defaced the club, but he could just as easily be talking about God himself. *You don't worry about him.*

"Because Daddy's going to fix it?" I ask, only the hint of a challenge. I'm a shadow of the girl I was in that club. Stripped of my armor. "Are you also going to buy me a mockingbird? And a diamond ring?"

"Do you want them?" he asks mildly.

Part of me wants to hit him, just to get a reaction. Something intense. Something meaningful. It's the same reason I smoked and drank and danced up against guys at dark underground parties. I lashed out at him, and God, he lashed back. "No."

"What do you want then?"

My gaze finds the black rectangle on the table again. It's been so long since I saw a Bible. Since I touched one. It leaves me shaken, and I want something other than a spanking. "Something to call mine."

I place one hand on his shoulder. He's tense underneath his suit jacket.

Slowly, carefully I climb into his lap. I half expect

him to mock me. Or maybe just push me to the ground. He doesn't do either of those things. He just lets me climb onto him, *into* him, cradling myself with his strong body, self-soothing with the erection I feel growing beneath his slacks.

One minute passes. Then another.

I've resigned myself to this, to holding him while he doesn't hold me back. Then his arm moves. He slides a hand around my shoulders and drapes his other arm over my legs. I'm curled up in his arms—like a child. That's how I feel, helpless and small.

Only now can I tell him what I've been thinking, ever since I saw the blood on the wall. Before that. When I saw the bubblegum-pink message on my vanity mirror. "It might be…" My voice breaks, and I have to start over again. "It might be someone from my past."

He's silent. I haven't talked much about my past. He saw me at the beginning, so he knows how sheltered I was, how warped. But he doesn't know the details. "Because of the Bible verses."

"Yes, and I need to go. I already planned on leaving, but it's even more important that I go now. Before he… before he hurts anyone."

Ivan's hands tighten on me. "Let's get one thing straight. You're not going anywhere. Not out of Tanglewood. And I might not even let you out of this house."

"You don't know what he's capable of," I whisper.

Ivan makes a low sound of disbelief—disbelief that I'd think he could be scared. "Whatever he's done, I've done worse. And I'll *do* worse if he's the one behind this. But you know, the Bible's kind of a popular book. Just because you knew some religious fuckhead before, doesn't mean he's here now."

That makes me laugh, despite myself. Ivan is always like this, irreverent. He doesn't give a shit about politeness. I wanted to be like him from the beginning. I never quite succeeded, could never quite lose the sense of wonder and fear that marks me as a sheep.

"They're both about the flock," I say. "And the shepherd."

Ivan tucks me against his chest, his chin on top of my head. "More than one man has delusions of grandeur. In fact, pretty much all of them do."

The thump of his heart in his chest is making me sleepy. "Even you?"

A huff of laughter. "Especially me. Why do you think I haven't touched you?"

I'm too tired, too broken to be anything but honest. "Because I'm dirty," I whisper.

It's what Leader Allen always said about my mother. *She has demons inside her. They drive men to sin. You won't let them in, will you, Candace? You'll be a good girl.*

Tension runs through Ivan's body in waves. His voice is even when he speaks. "I don't know who made you believe that. But I'd love five minutes in a room with him."

"Then why?" I ask, my voice sluggish in sleep. *Why haven't you touched me?*

"I'm not sure it matters anymore."

CHAPTER ELEVEN

H E CARRIES ME upstairs. I'm drifting on the shore between sleep and waking, content to remain here as long as I feel his arms around me. As long as I can smell his musk. *As long as I'm safe.*

The sheets are cold against my heated skin, and I make a negative sound.

He starts to pull away, and I grab on to him. It's so cold in this room. So colorless. "Please," I beg.

He stares down at me in the dark, more shadow than man. "Go to sleep."

"I won't," I say, but that's a lie. I'm already half-asleep even while we talk, pulled further out on every wave—and he's sand between my fingers. Even knowing that, I hold him tighter. "I'll have nightmares."

"Shhh," he says, and relief fills me.

"You'll stay?"

"Shhh," he says again, and I know the answer is no.

The bed shifts as he sits on the edge. He strokes my temple, my cheek. "So pretty," he says, and I shiver. I never wanted to be pretty. I never wanted to drive men to sin—until that was all I had left.

His hand strokes lower, down my neck, and over the

swell of my breasts. I suck in a breath. This is the most he's ever touched me. His fingers are light, barely a caress. It's more like he's tracing me under my clothes. This is as far as he's ever gone with me. That may sound strange considering I've had my panties down while he spanked me, but nothing else ever happened. Now we're in a bed and he's touching my body. My hands lie on the bed, not stopping him.

When he reaches my panties, he slips his hand inside.

My whole body flushes hot and then prickles with goose bumps. I bow up off the bed, a soft sound escaping me. "Ivan? What are you—"

"No, Candy. You know better than that."

The thud of my heart almost drowns out his words. Almost. I know what he wants from me. I just don't know if I can give it to him. I move to push him away.

He presses one wrist down on the bed. "Don't fight me, little one."

I close my eyes on a deep breath. No, I can do this. God, I've practically begged him for this. Now that he's finally giving it to me, I'm afraid. It's too much, his calluses on my bare flesh, the contrast of my pale peach panties stretched taut over his large hand.

He seems to be resting there, not moving. I push my hips into his touch, but he squeezes my wrist and lets it go. "No," he says gently. "You need to be a good girl now."

My mouth forms the words without making a sound. "Yes, Daddy."

The shift is subtle, just a twist of corded muscles. Then his fingers are on my clit, *around* my clit, forefinger and middle finger sliding on either side. Exactly how I touch myself. He's watched me do it in that basement. He's studied me, and now he uses that knowledge against me.

Pleasure pours through my body, molten hot, and I moan softly.

It's more than the way he touches me. It's how hard he presses, how fast he goes. Every second I spent under him, obeying him, he knew exactly what I was doing. And I know that he was telling the truth down in the dining room. He never did ignore me. Of all the things he did to me, he never did that.

I'm flat on my back, hands bound at my sides because he told me to. My legs are spread just enough for him to touch me. Completely at his mercy.

He rubs faster, and I can't help myself now. I squirm against his touch, trying to get myself off. "Does it feel good?" he murmurs.

Of course he knows the answer, and even more so when I pant, "Yes, Daddy. *Please.*"

"You'll get there, little one. I'm going to help you."

I don't know what that means until I feel cool air over my tummy. He lifts my tank top higher until my breasts are exposed. My breasts aren't small, but his hand covers one completely, plumping it and caressing me until I'm shaking. I'm on fire both inside and out, the flames of my arousal licking me inside, his hands like a brand on my pussy and breasts.

"I feel funny, Daddy," I say, my voice trembling. "I feel…"

"I know. That's your body's way of helping you relax."

"I don't—I don't feel relaxed." I feel strung up tight, every muscle in my body hard and tense. I know what an orgasm is, I've given myself plenty of them, but this is different. Those were stars in the sky, far away and almost invisible. This is like the sun, making me burn. I'm sweating, panting. Begging. "Help me. I can't…"

"Shh. I am helping you. But you have to let it happen. You have to give in."

He pinches my clit at the same time as he pinches my nipple, and the heat consumes me completely. I cry out as my climax overtakes me, scorching me, hurting me more than anything, until my body douses the fire, gushing my release over his hand and drenching my panties.

I'm still gasping for breath when he pulls away.

Two fingers push at my mouth, and I open for him instinctively. "Clean them," he says softly, and I taste the musk of my own release. He rests his palm on my chin, keeping his fingers inside me. I slide my tongue over him, the ridges of his calluses sending sparks through my body.

"Good little girls like to suck, don't they?"

I nod without releasing him, my eyes wide. I would suck more than his fingers, and he must know that. He makes no move to undo his pants—to fuck me or to let me suck him. He just keeps his fingers in my mouth, casual and perverse, letting me take comfort from the fullness.

There are questions I want to ask him. Things I need to say.

But I don't want him to move his hand, so I continue sucking, taking my reward for being such a good girl. I let him touch me. *You have to give in.* And I do that, if only for one night. That's how I fall asleep, with his steady breathing as my lullaby, his thumb caressing my cheek, his fingers resting on my tongue.

CHAPTER TWELVE

I DREAM OF volcanos, of giant explosions and the drifting of ash. I see red molten rivers that turn black. The earth cracks open, swallows us whole, reclaiming what it had lost.

I feel the singe of my skin, smell burned flesh. I hear the screams—and I sit up.

My screams. I pant, trying to gather myself. I heard myself scream. The sheets are tangled around my waist. The room is empty. I wait in the inky night, almost expecting Ivan to burst in the room. Won't he have heard me?

Maybe he's deep in sleep. Or more likely, maybe his bedroom is far away from here, on the other side of this massive house with thick walls. His room is on the third floor. I know that much, but he never let me in there. Not in the year that I lived here, and sure as hell not last night. The first and only time I tried to explore it as a naive sixteen-year-old, I actually got lost. When Ivan found me, he sternly marched me downstairs with strict instructions never to return.

He treats me like a child, and I obey him, because I like it.

I still like it, but not enough to stay.

I need more than that.

Part of me is disappointed he didn't hear. I want to see what he'd do to comfort me, what else he might give me to suck. Another part of me knows this is for the best. This is my chance.

I cross the room and find my cell phone in the pocket of my jeans. The light blinds me for a second before I can make a call.

One ring. Two.

"Hello?"

"Clara. It's me. Candy."

"Yeeeah," she says, drawing out the word, sounding distracted. "They have this thing called caller ID. I saw it was you before I answered."

"Mhm, thanks for the technology lesson, but actually I need your help with something else."

I can feel her attention snap to me over the line. "Something wrong?"

That means she hasn't heard about the blood at the Grand. That's good. If she knew, she might be more inclined to side with Ivan about this. "I need you to pick me up from Fourth and Lennox in twenty minutes."

"Are you in trouble? Should I bring Kip?"

Clara is the little sister of Honor, one of the girls who used to dance at the club. When Honor got into trouble, Clara spent a couple of hours at the Grand under my questionable supervision. We struck up something resembling a friendship, even though I have no business talking to someone that innocent. Not anymore.

Kip is Honor's very protective, very dangerous husband. He'd be only too happy to protect me, but it would put them all at risk.

It would also eventually get back to Ivan.

"Tell no one," I say, doing my best stern-elder impression. Even though I'm only one year older than her.

"Okay, Ms. Mysterious. I'll be there."

"Are you coming from home? Head down I-32 and exit at—"

"They also have this thing called maps. Like on phones. And—"

"Smart-ass," I say, but I can't help but smile. Even in the midst of all this, deep in the heart of a torn up city, she's a breath of fresh air.

I hang up with a sense of anticipation and dread. Anticipation because I have a lot to do in twenty minutes. I have to sneak out of Ivan's house, which is almost as hard as sneaking in. Of course I have the advantage of knowing most of his pass codes and Luca's habits.

And dread because now I have to leave Ivan, for real. Maybe I always knew he would fight me when I told him I'd leave. Maybe I always hoped it would lead to something like last night, where he'd finally touch me. Finally treat me like a woman.

Now I'm leaving forever, and he's not here to stop me. I know this is for the best. I need to stay one step ahead of the man who's after me—and more importantly, my presence here will put everyone in danger.

I'm also disobeying Ivan, and deep inside, that feels like the worst sin of all.

✧   ✧   ✧

I'M SOAKING WET by the time I reach Fourth and Lennox. It turns out there *is* a moat. Who knew?

Okay, it's more like a drainage ditch, but it accomplished the same thing. Now I'm shivering in wet jeans while I huddle against the brick building. My phone gave up the fight with the water. At least no one will be able to track me with it. I toss it into a gutter before melting back into the shadows.

I'm still in the upscale side of Tanglewood, near where Ivan lives, so I don't want to be seen. A woman without a car or a man nearby would definitely stand out.

The cherry-red hatchback pulls to a stop at the curb, and I hop inside. "Hey."

Clara gives me a look that says she's going to need more of an explanation than that. Fair enough. She deserves some answers, but I'm going to have to be careful. The more she knows, the more likely she is to go digging, asking more questions when I'm gone, getting herself into trouble.

"So, where are we going?" she says, as casual as if we were going to hang out at the mall. And now I'm suddenly depressed that we never got to hang out at the mall. It would have been sweet to do something normal, for her and for me. We both grew up sheltered. We had that in common.

"We're going to the truck stop down I-32. That's where you get off this ride."

She doesn't seem surprised about that. Just worried. "I'm supposed to leave you in the middle of nowhere?"

"No," I say patiently. "At a truck stop. That's somewhere."

Her eyes flash. "And if you get killed, I'm supposed to be okay with that?"

"I'm not going to get killed." Not that she would find out if I did. At the very least I'll vanish before my hypothetical murder takes place. "Anyway, this isn't...it's not a game. It's not a party."

She knows about my party habits. Well, everyone does. Not to brag, but I'm kind of infamous for it. I think Clara even guessed why I did it for so long. We're very different, the wild stripper and the quiet artist, but we have certain things in common.

Worry enters her eyes. "If it's not a game, then what is it?"

"I'm leaving. For good." And because I know she'll argue, I add softly, "I have to."

She opens her mouth and then closes it. She must have figured out that an emotional denial wouldn't sway me. Smart girl. I glance toward the backseat. Her backpack is half-open, rolled up paper peeking out from the zipper.

"Shit," I say. "Were you at the studio or some shit?"

She rents space in some kind of studio co-op so she

has space for her large sculptures.

"At two o'clock in the morning?" She sounds amused. "They aren't even open."

"How the hell would I know?" I sigh. "I'm the worst influence. I shouldn't have called. You were probably sketching. Or you know, sleeping."

"Something like that," she mutters.

I've hit a nerve. "What's wrong?"

"Nothing," she says, obviously lying.

I'm torn between curiosity and a strange protective desire to hide her away from the world. Is this what Ivan feels about me? No wonder he always looks like he has a stick up his ass. It's maddening. "Clara."

She snorts. "So you can keep your secrets, secrets which might get you *hurt,* secrets that mean I won't ever get to see you again after tonight, but I have to tell you everything I'm thinking."

I hear the pain in her voice, and my heart squeezes. "I didn't think you would miss me," I whisper.

Her hands tighten on the steering wheel. "Well, why not? I thought we were friends. Won't you miss me?"

It kills me how open she is with her emotions, how free she is with her affection. She grew up in a cold environment and then had to live on the run for months. She should have been hardened by now, like me. "I'm kind of annoying, that's why," I say lightly. "I call you up at two in the morning and make you drive around the city."

"It's part of your charm," she says ruefully.

I've never called her out in the middle of the night before, but I'm not a chat-over-tea kind of person either. "I will miss you," I tell my reflection in the car window, unable to face her.

Her hand is warm on my arm. "Will you please tell me what's wrong? Maybe you don't have to leave. Maybe there's some kind of solution to whatever it is. Is it money?"

I shake my head. There's only a few bucks in my jeans pocket. I have a much larger stash back at my apartment, but I can't risk going back. Ivan has stationed men all around there. I survived on twenty dollars when I was sixteen years old. I can do it again.

"Is it—" Her voice cracks. "Is it Ivan?"

Clara has always been nervous about him, which is understandable. She's nervous about all men, which is also understandable considering what happened to her when she was younger.

"It's not him," I say, "but you can't tell him you saw me tonight."

She gives me an insulted look. "Duh."

I know she'll be loyal to me. It's one of the reasons I called her and not anyone else. Even Lola, who's probably my best friend, would crack under the pressure once Ivan started questioning her. Besides, I don't want to cause a rift between her and her fiancé, Blue, whose company manages security at the Grand. But actually no one really knows that Clara and I kept in touch. I'm counting on that. There won't be any trail for Ivan to follow.

CHAPTER THIRTEEN

I T'S RAINING BY the time we reach the truck stop and say our goodbyes. Clara doesn't want to leave me here, but in the end she's solemn and dry-eyed. The heavy knowledge looks strange on her sweet, almost babyish face. I watch the taillights disappear before I turn my attention to the inventory.

I'm humming "It's Raining Men" under my breath as I size up each rig and driver. I get a few catcalls, some offers of cash for sex. One is particularly colorful, offering to wash up first.

Charming.

Most of the men here are little more than animals. They'd take what they want from me if given the chance, whether I consented or not. Only the thinnest veneer of manners keeps them from surrounding me right here in the parking lot. They could take me down—a full pack against one weakened gazelle.

Luckily, I have a lot of experience training lions. I'm a fucking ringmaster.

Head high. Don't show any fear. Walk like you own everything you can see.

I find the one I need near the back, in one of the

shittier parking spots. He's a little young. Definitely horny. And the way he looks at me tells me everything I need to know. He admires me, he wants me. But most of all he looks up to me, the way I look up to Ivan. This one wouldn't offer me sixty bucks to suck his dick, clean or otherwise. And he'd never force me. Hell, he'd probably give me all the money from his wallet if I asked him to. He'd beg me to refuse him an orgasm. *Perfect.*

"Give a girl a ride?" I ask.

He licks his lips, looking from side to side. Nope, no one is standing right next to his rig but him. "Where you heading?"

"Where you going?"

"Gainesville," he says too quickly. God, he'd be a dream to train. If only…

"Then that's where I'm heading," I say with a smile.

He nearly trips over himself to clean the cab of his truck in the minutes before we leave. It's exactly what I'd expect from him. Fast-food wrappers and porn magazines with women in leather. The industrial-grade lights in the parking lot illuminate his blush as he shoves everything under the seat.

I put my hand on his arm. We need to get out of here sooner rather than later. As in, right freaking now. Ivan will be coming after me when he notices I'm gone. More than that, I'm worried about whoever left those messages at the Grand. I don't think I've been followed here, but it never hurts to be careful.

Most of all, I'm a little nervous about the other

truckers who are gathering around us.

"Hey, mister. This is real nice. Thank you for making me comfortable." I give his arm a little squeeze. "But I wonder if we could get going now?"

"Oh, right!" He looks around at the men who've advanced on us, just a few feet away from the truck. They aren't making a rush for us, and I heard the locks click. But at least one of those men is packing heat, and I really don't want to test these windows. Apparently my little subbie trucker doesn't either. He guns the engine, and we speed into the night.

MY CHAUFFER'S NAME is Charlie, and he's from Kentucky. He's driving his uncle's rig, since his uncle broke his leg playing street hockey. I can't figure out if that's a euphemism for something.

I let Charlie ramble and blush and stammer. He's really a sweetheart. Once we're ten miles out, he stops for some food and drinks. I slurp on a huge tub of soda and watch him drive.

"So, Charlie." I draw out his name, infusing it with the kind of sultry sound that earns me double the tips at the Grand. "Do you have a girl back home?"

"N-no," he says, and I believe him. At least, I believe he doesn't have the girl. But he wants one.

"What's her name?"

"Alyssa," he says, then turns beet red. A-freaking-dorable. "But I'm not—we're not—"

"It's okay, Charlie. I understand. Unrequited love is a bitch." I understand more than I want to. People act like love is a gift, but it's not. It's theft. It's a goddamn tragedy.

Love is losing a vital organ to a man who will never give his in return.

Charlie studies the black expanse, dotted with red and white and yellow. "I figure if I can get my own rig, she might look at me different."

"Older or younger?" I ask.

"She's older," he says. "But I don't mind."

"Of course you don't," I assure him. He prefers it, actually. "And what does she do for a living?"

If I thought he was red before, now he is an actual tomato. "She's a…well, she's a stripper. But she doesn't, you know. It's not like that."

Oh dear. I have a feeling I know exactly what it's like. Alyssa does her job very well. That's what it's like. "Well, I don't know Alyssa, but I'm absolutely sure that one day you will find the perfect woman for you. One who loves you. One who understands you. One who will tell you exactly what to do to please her."

His eyes grew wide, a mixture of shock and arousal swirling in his light brown eyes. "You really think so?"

I'm saved by having to reply by the earsplitting whoop of a siren. A second later blue and red lights bounce off the tall columns of rearview mirrors on either side.

"Shit," Charlie says, fumbling for the blinker. "I wasn't even speeding."

I narrow my eyes at the cruiser as we pull over, bouncing on the rough interstate shoulder. "I don't think they're here for you."

"Oh fuck," Charlie breathes. "Are you in trouble? Should we make a run for it?"

I soften. "Charlie, you'll make a really amazing boyfriend one day. And to do that, you need to not be dead. So no, don't make a run for anything. Just sit there and do whatever the cops say."

We don't have to wait long. The cop that comes up to the window is familiar. He shines his flashlight inside, taking in both of us. At least he doesn't flash it in my eyes. "Good evening," he says in that drawl of his. I really hate that fucking drawl.

"It's morning," I say, annoyed. "Aren't we a little outside your jurisdiction, Officer?"

He just smiles. *Creep.*

That's the thing about bribing cops. All the ones who'll accept bribes are total assholes. "I'm outta here," I say, blowing a kiss to Charlie. "You go ahead."

His mouth is open. "But—"

I smile and slam the door against his bewildered expression. It would only be worse for him if he hung around. Officer Asshole bangs the door and tells him to drive away. When he's back in the flow of traffic, I start walking.

"Hey," Officer Asshole shouts. "Where are you going?"

I shoot him the finger and keep walking.

CHAPTER FOURTEEN

IVAN SHOWS UP an hour later. I'm simultaneously annoyed that he took this long and annoyed that he showed up at all. The limo pulls to a stop a few hundred feet ahead of me, leaving me with the awkward choice of walking straight toward him or turning around.

"Let's get this over with," I mutter to myself.

Ivan steps out and leans against the car. The walk is longer than it looks, and he watches me the whole time. I watch him right back, taking in his broad shoulders and trim waist. The cut of his suit is the kind only ten thousand dollars can buy, custom designed to contour his powerful body. No doubt the gravel being kicked up by the eight-lane highway would ruin his Italian leather oxfords.

At least the shoulder is wide enough that I can walk in relative safety. Zooming cars create a wall of light and noise. Night blocks us in from the other side, and it forms an intimate hallway for the two of us. The sun is just peeking over the horizon, casting a weirdly romantic sepia glow.

Up close, I can feel the fury emanating from him. That's okay. I'm angry too.

"How?" I bite out.

His expression is made of marble, his voice pure steel. "You don't want to do this here."

I laugh, which is kind of like waving a red flag in front of a bull. But I'm feeling just that reckless at the moment. I've left my home of three years with nothing but a few folded bills in my pocket, all so I can be safe. And now I don't even have that much. "And you know what I want? If you want me to get in that car, you're going to have to tell me *how.*"

He's silent while my mind fills in the blanks. Did he follow me all the way from his house? I don't think so. I've gotten pretty good at evading his security measures—and his men. That's what he gets for having them tail me all the time. I know how to lose them.

Did Clara give me up? I didn't think she would, but obviously something went wrong.

"Your phone," he says between gritted teeth.

I spread my hands. "I don't have one anymore. It died. I tossed it."

"Not a tracker," he says after a minute.

"Ivan…" I know he doesn't want to give up his secrets. But he doesn't want to bodily force me into the car either, not with all these witnesses. Not when there's still a chance I could run away. He doesn't have any particular desire to run across eight packed lanes, but in my darker moments, I do.

"A tap," he says.

Surprise and anger and the smallest bit of hurt battle

in my chest. "You listened to my conversations?"

"Not all of them."

In other words, a lot of them. "Fuck you, Ivan. Really just…fuck you. And you wonder why I don't trust you. So you know Clara picked me up."

In one fluid motion he grabs my wrist and twists my arm behind my back. The front of my body slams against the car where he'd been leaning. The metal is still warm from his body.

His voice is low by my ear. "Yes, we knew she picked you up. She wouldn't tell us anything when we found her, but her phone history led us to the truck stop. Every man there remembered the pretty little girl wandering around. For the right price they gave up which truck she was in and which way they were headed."

Of course they did. The cars whiz by, no one stopping to check on the girl being held against her will. No one wants to fuck with Ivan, even people who don't know his reputation. It's in the way he holds himself.

"You're hurting me," I whimper.

He twists harder. "Is that enough information for you? Or do you need me to draw you a fucking diagram?"

"You should have let me go." My voice is muffled against the car, thick from unshed tears. "I didn't want to be found. I wanted to disappear."

He pulls me back only enough to push me into the car. I stumble onto the leather seats and curl into a ball. "Congratulations," he says, his voice toneless and cruel.

"You've got your wish. You're going to disappear from the side of the road tonight, and no one will ever find you."

Chapter Fifteen

IVAN IS SILENT on the ride home, but that silence speaks volumes. I hear what a bad girl I am, how he'll punish me. I know it won't be like before—a spanking while I finger myself. That's way too generous for how he feels right now. It will be something bad.

What do you want? More money? More pain? Should I start using a cane on you?

He asked me that. And I might find out what a cane feels like today. Or worse.

I'm angry too. Angry that he found me, that he's dragging me back. But it's hard to hold on to that in the face of my fear. I never really wanted him to hurt me. I already feel torn up inside, flayed with the barbed-wire bonds of love for a man who can never return it. It's hard to imagine he can make me feel worse than I already do.

I can count on his determination to find a way.

"Upstairs," he says as soon as we walk in the door.

It's blazing daylight outside, but in his house it's like we're down in the basement. The windows are tightly sealed, shutters and blinds and curtains locking out the cheery sun. The only light comes from overhead, recessed lighting that leads the way to my room.

My room. I slept here for a year before I convinced Ivan to let me dance at the club and could afford my own place, such as it was. And in that year I never put up a picture, never painted a wall. Never did anything that would mark the bare walls as my own.

I stand in the center of the room, waiting.

He stops at the door, his eyes hard and glittering like diamonds. "No."

I raise my eyebrows. "No?"

He nods toward the stairs. *Keep going.* The third floor.

The place he never let me go.

My heart beats faster at the realization that he might tear that wall down.

I take a step toward the door. "Your room?"

"Yes." He doesn't seem pleased about it. No, he seems furious. "That's what you wanted, isn't it? To sleep in my bed and suck on my cock."

I flinch at the crude words. It is what I wanted, but he makes it sound dirty. No, he makes it sound sinful. And it is a sin. That's all I'm made of, sin after sin, sewn together with a string of desire.

"Move," he says shortly, and I know he's going to make this as painful as possible.

I climb the stairs with trembling legs, clinging to the railing so I don't trip and fall. He's right behind me. I know he'd catch me. He'd drag me up to the room if he had to.

At the landing, I don't know which way to go. "At

the end," he says, nodding to the right.

The room is massive, but it's only fitting, considering the bed. There's a heavy-looking dresser. Other than that, it's sparse. Kind of like my room one floor down.

"Strip," he says.

I face him, understanding dawning. This is his punishment for running away. He's going to give me exactly what I've always wanted—sex with him. I wanted that because then he'd be treating me like a woman. Like an equal. Only, he's not going to do it like that. He's going to do it painful and cruel. He's going to make it hurt.

My hands can barely work the button on my jeans, and I shove them down. There's no grace now. He's seen me dance onstage. He knows what I look like, practiced, seductive. He's never seen me like this, falling apart. I've never *felt* like this. Even the first time I met him, afraid and alone, I had determination. I had hope. Now I don't even have that.

You're going to disappear from the side of the road tonight, and no one will ever find you.

I take off my tank top and drop it to the floor. Now I'm completely naked.

And he has all his clothes on. I want him to take them off, but I know he won't. He doesn't ever. And besides, that wouldn't make it a punishment.

"Ivan," I whisper.

"On the bed."

My eyelids fall shut and push the gathering tears down my cheeks. "Ivan."

"No?" he asks. A hand clamps onto my wrist, pulling me across the room. "All right then. The dresser. Bend over."

I don't really have a choice, the way he throws me against it. I catch myself on my palms. The sound of a zipper comes from behind me, and I look over my shoulder. I can't see anything, but I can feel it. God, he's already lined up against me.

I'm just repeating his name now, a plea and a prayer. "Ivan. Ivan, please."

I brace myself for the pain, but then he's gone. His fingers press against my pussy, almost as blunt and far more rough. They slide along my folds, feeling my slickness.

He chuckles. "Do you want this, little one? Your body says yes."

I've never done this. I'm a virgin. Please don't hurt me.

The words catch in my throat. His fingers are on my clit, rubbing me from behind. I groan and rock my hips into his touch. It's the only relief I feel, the only relief I've ever felt. He fondles roughly, which only seems to drive me higher. My legs are like jelly. The only things holding me up are my hands on the dresser and his fingers on my clit.

I don't think he knows I've never done this, not with how rough he's being. He must think I gave it up sometime in the club or at one of the parties. His fingers are too fast, too hard, and I'm on the brink of orgasm, hovering on the razor's edge. He takes his hand away, and the loss is a physical pain, sharp and cold.

"This is what you wanted," he says. "You think I didn't know the way you looked at me? Fuck, you looked at me like that the first fucking night I met you, and you didn't even know what it meant."

He pushes the head of his cock against my slickness. *Oh God.*

The memories come back to me. I slept in the same room as my mother, on a mat on the floor. The room was connected to Leader Allen's. He would wake her in the middle of the night, bring her to his room. The door was open. I could hear everything. And sometimes, when I crawled across the floor, see everything.

Kneel, he would tell her. And she would get on her knees beside the bed and pray. When she was done, when she had begged forgiveness, he would lift her up enough so her body was half on the bed. Then he would pull up his robes and—

A sharp pain presses me open, and I gasp. It hurts too much to speak, hurts too much to cry. My body is rejecting him, pushing him out—and losing the fight. I hold on to the dresser like my life depends on it, but it won't matter. I'm being split apart. I can't imagine I'll survive it, but at least when I die, it will be over. It feels like my whole body is impaled.

Rough hands grab my hips, thick fingers bruising flesh. Another push and he's farther in. God, how is there more? A sob finally escapes me.

"*Ivan.*"

"You're so fucking tight," he says between clenched teeth. "How the fuck are you so tight?"

My inner muscles clench and release, fighting his entrance every step of the way. I couldn't relax them even if I wanted to. The burn is too much, the stretch is too wide. I pant against the dresser, my hands clasped together, praying for it to end.

"I've never—" My breath is coming too fast. Blackness is closing in. It's like in the basement, except his hands aren't around my throat. No, this time his cock is pushing inside my pussy—and it's even worse. I can't breathe, can hardly speak. "Never done this before."

He freezes.

A long minute passes where the only thing I can feel is the throb of his cock, and the only thing I can see is black. I'm still conscious—barely. I'm panting, struggling to keep breathing, to stay here with him. To experience this thing I've wanted for so long, even if it's the worst thing that's ever happened to me.

"What did you say?" His voice sounds far away again, but strangely controlled. Completely unlike how he sounded two minutes ago, his fury uncontained.

In a painful wrench, he removes himself—it somehow hurts worse than it did going in, the salt of him stinging the tears in my skin. Without his hands or his cock, I collapse on the ground, leaning against the dresser. My hands are covering my sex, protective, though they do nothing to take away the pain.

A hand fists in my hair and pulls. I'm facing him,

looking up at him while he looms over me. He's still wearing his suit, his cock hard and jutting out. It's an angry red from arousal, tinged glossy and pink with my blood. And it's terrifying. It would have scared me if I had seen it anytime, but now that I know how much it can hurt, I'm even more scared.

He gives me a little shake by my hair. "What did you say?"

My throat feels raw, as if I've been screaming even though I haven't. "I'm a virgin," I whisper.

Or at least I used to be.

Chapter Sixteen

I ALWAYS THOUGHT it was a little ironic, my virginity. My so-called virtue. I should have been keeping it safe to save my immortal soul, but the truth is I assume I've already lost any chance at heaven. I'm far from innocent regardless of what has or hasn't been inside my pussy. I've given men lap dances, seen their come stain their pants as they explode. I've even fooled around with guys at parties, flirted and almost fucked.

Ivan's expression is more angry than incredulous. "How the fuck is that possible?"

I manage a watery laugh, my voice somehow wry through my tears. "I'm a cock tease, Ivan. I thought you knew that about me."

His hands curl into fists. "What the fuck were you saving yourself for? For marriage? For love?"

He sounds almost more disgusted by the idea of love than he is by marriage. "Maybe."

The truth is I was saving myself for *him*, but I can't deny his words. I did want him to love me, to marry me, even while I understood how impossible that was. I have a long history of wanting the impossible. I wanted Ivan to love me, even though he doesn't understand the meaning of the word. He's made of ice. I wanted to feel powerful with my body, even though most of the men who come through our doors would hold me down and fuck me if they got the chance.

And most of all, I wanted to be free from my past, free from Harmony Hills and its scriptures. Now that someone is leaving Bible verses at the Grand, I know I will never be free. Not only from a man, but from the teachings I thought I'd left behind.

"It's too late now," he says, his tone indecipherable.

I look down between my legs, where my hands are still cupped protectively. *Too late.* "Yes."

His hand fists his cock, stroking once, twice. "I hope you don't think I'm going to take it easy on you because of this."

Fear tightens my throat as I watch him. "It hurt too much. It's too big."

"Not too big. Your body was designed to take men. To take *me*. Now get on the bed."

I scramble to the bed, skirting him as far as I can, as if his cock might reach out and impale me while I'm not looking.

I'm sore between my legs. It was only a dull throb when I sat on the floor, but when I move, it's so much worse, fire licking me from inside. It wasn't just precum from *his* body that stung my cuts and tears. It's my own wetness too, because I can't deny how he makes me feel. Even when I'm hurting, when I'm dying from the pain of him stretching me, breaking me, I want him.

That's how we are together—depraved and beautiful.

I scramble beneath the covers, hiding my body, the cool sheets a thin barrier.

He studies me, his expression softening a fraction. But if I thought it would make him gentle, I'd be wrong. He grasps the corner of the sheet and pulls. It slinks to the ground, leaving me bare. Cool air washes over me.

One large hand circles my ankle. That's the only warning I have before he pulls me toward him. Then I'm sprawled on the bed, legs open to his view. "I didn't prepare you before," he says, and it's the closest he will ever come to an apology.

Then he bends his head, and I gasp. "What—"

My voice is choked off when his lips find my clit, a gentle kiss. Pleasure arcs through me, and I twist my body. "No, wait," I tell him. "Wait."

He lifts his head only slightly, raising one eyebrow. I can read his expression. He has no intention of stopping because I want him to, but he's curious about what I'm going to say. I'm curious too, because I don't even know. I can't even think. My brain shorted out the second his mouth touched my sex.

"I'm—I'm bleeding," I tell him. There's blood on his cock, and it's mine.

Amusement flits over his face. "You think because there's blood on your pussy, I can't lick you?"

"Yes," I whisper. A flush makes my face hot to hear him say the words, to even think about him tasting me— tasting my arousal, tasting my blood.

His expression hardens. "It's mine, Candy. Your blood, your body. Your virginity. You belong to me now. You don't get to tell me no. And if you think I'm not going to fuck you, or lick you, or do anything I damn well please because of a little blood, then you have a lot to learn, little one."

Then his head dips again, and it's like electricity zings from the base of my sex up to the top of my clit. He presses his tongue against my hole, soothing the place that he hurt, making it burn even more.

The soft fabric of his suit whispers against the insides of my thighs. Rough fingers play with my folds before they hold me open for his assault. His tongue is wet and hot and knowledgeable as it flicks me, using just the right rhythm. My hips rock up to meet him. Unforgiving hands press my thighs down, forcing me flat on the bed.

He focuses on my clit, merciless as he lashes me again and again.

I clutch the sheets and twist my upper body, my legs held down by him. The orgasm hits me like a tidal wave, pushing me under and stealing my breath. I can't even cry out, can't beg or scream. I can only jerk my body against the bonds of his hands as the orgasm drags on and on. My lungs burn from lack of air. Even then he doesn't let up, his tongue dipping into my hole, drinking the juices I make for him.

Only when he pulls back can I finally suck in air— and let it out on a pitiful wail.

My defenses are broken, battered. He tore them

down with single-minded intent, and now what's left of me? I want him to do it again. More than that, I want him to be naked while he does it. I want him to be as vulnerable as I am, as open to me as I am to him.

Clumsy hands push at his suit jacket. "Take it off," I say brokenly. "Take it—"

Gray eyes narrow. "Stop, Candace."

He hitches the head of his cock against my pussy. My whole body goes tense, knowing exactly how much it will hurt. "No. Don't. Please."

"Excuse me?"

"Take it off." I'm begging, pleading. I don't really want him to stop. Even if he splits me in two pieces, I want him to do it. I just want him to be naked when he does it. Naked with me. Intimate. "At least the suit jacket. Please."

He tenses up, clearly angry. "Stop asking for that. You won't like what happens."

That again. "You don't know what I like," I cry. "You don't."

I think that's a lie. We both know it. The way he just played my body, his tongue against my clit, proves he knows exactly what I like. The way I came, so hard my body almost broke under the strain, proves it too.

He laughs, an almost metallic sound. "You want me to take my clothes off."

My voice is shaky. "Yes."

"You want me to strip for you?"

"Yes." Stronger now.

A knowing expression lights his pale eyes as his hands go to his lapels. He looks dangerous like this, almost insane with it. It makes me scared for what I'll see underneath. I never thought his clothes were anything more than a wall between us. I never even realized they might be armor, the same way ruffles and glitter have been for me.

He takes off the jacket in rough, careless movements. It drops to the floor in a whisper of expensive fabric. The shirt comes next, one button at a time. His eyes never leave mine. There's challenge in them. He expects me to balk. *But why?*

When all the buttons are undone, he opens each cuff. Then he shrugs off the shirt.

It joins the jacket on the floor, but I can't focus on that. Not with his chest bared to me.

Not with the scars.

They steal my breath away. There are too many scars to count, a patchwork quilt of pain. A lifetime of war and abuse. Some of the girls at the Grand came from rough backgrounds. Some of the customers too. So I recognize the small, circular marks as cigarette burns. They are old and faded and poignant. Crisscrossing them are slashes—knife wounds? Not straight enough for that. Maybe the torn edge of a beer can. Or the jagged blade of a broken bottle.

He hasn't stopped moving under my perusal. He takes off his belt buckle and pushes down his pants, then his boxer briefs, too proud to flinch when I see what's underneath. I flinch though, and let out a sound of pure, undiluted horror.

The scars don't stop at his waist. They continue down, over lean hips and muscular thighs. Cuts and burns and dark, disfigured patches where I don't even know what happened. It's such a contrast to his smooth, cultured appearance in his bespoke suits that my mind can't really comprehend what I'm seeing. This is more than fistfights. More even than the gun and knife warfare of criminals. This is torture. Long-term torture from many years ago.

When he could have only been a child.

My eyes fill with tears. "Oh God, Ivan."

"No," he says roughly. "You wanted to see this. A monster fucking you."

"Daddy—"

He covers my mouth with his hand, cutting off my plea.

Then his cock is pushing into me, spearing me slowly but inexorably. My muscles flutter and clench against the invasion. It hurts just as much the second time—more, somehow. I feel my eyes go wide and then fill with tears. My body jerks against his weight, fighting him, completely involuntary as I push him away.

I don't mean to fight though. As much as it hurts. As much as it burns. I wouldn't say a single word to stop him from doing this. Not after seeing what pain he's endured. This can never be worse than that.

His hand remains over my mouth as he presses in to

the hilt. The black hair at his base feels foreign against my bare pussy, scratchy against oversensitized skin. I'm dizzy with being this full, almost light-headed. I think his hand is blocking some of my air too, and I have to move. I don't mean to fight him, but my body does it for me, jerking against him, trying to squirm away and buck him off. I fight his hand too, pulling at it, trying to get more air. No matter how much I struggle, it doesn't work. He's too strong like this. Too determined. Too cruel.

A monster fucking you.

That's what he called himself, a monster. And that's how he seems. Not because of the scars I can see moving over me in a blur. Because of the light in his eyes, the one that says he'll make this hurt. It's a promise he makes, a promise he keeps as he pulls back and then plunges in again. There's no time to adjust to his size; he just starts fucking me. Pounding me. The pain over-whelms me, and I feel tears stream down the sides of my face, shockingly cool against the heat of my body.

I struggle in earnest now, using all my strength to push him off me. Because it's terrifying to see him this way, because it hurts worse than anything. Because I think he wants me to fight. I can almost hear his voice in my head. *That's what monsters do to pretty little girls.*

And pretty little girls are expected to fight.

I yank and pull at his arm, trying to dislodge it. I twist my hips, fighting to close my legs. None of it moves him. I'm trapped by his hand and his cock. Trapped by the relentless pain.

He could end this quickly.

He's waited so long to do it. Minutes, hours. Years. He could have come inside me and been done. That's not what monsters do. He'll make this last for just as long he wants it to. I could be held underneath him for eternity, feeling his cock spear into me, rubbing me raw.

His expression is torn, somehow both despairing and smug. I must seem like some kind of sacrificial lamb to him, a sacrifice on the altar of his wickedness.

It's how I feel as the pain consumes me, threatening to tear down my sanity. I think I might really be losing it. My sanity, my consciousness. I almost wish I could black out, so I wouldn't have to feel this. He could fuck my limp body until the end of time, and I wouldn't feel a thing.

The bed rolls with every thrust. The scent of our combined musk fills the air, along with the metal of my blood. It feels like I'm adrift on an angry ocean, and he's the storm bearing down on me. He batters me without a care for how I'm ripped apart and torn.

He closes his eyes against whatever he sees in my eyes, focused on his own pleasure now. He's in his own world, fucking me, using me, drenching his cock with me again and again.

His breathing is harsh, surrounding me. I listen to him breathe in and out, the sound pained. Tortured. Does this hurt him, fucking me forever? Or is he always hurting, the caress of my inner flesh a temporary reprieve from a lifetime of suffering?

His eyes fly open, and I see in them so many things—possession and hunger, anger and fear. He shouts into the huge room, and it echoes off the walls. He jerks roughly, losing his rhythm. Then again.

Then he stills, pushing and pulsing against my hips, his whole body trembling.

He stares into my eyes the entire time, letting me see everything inside him, a vortex that sucks me in deep. His cock flexes as he bathes my sex with warm come. It stings the newly stretched skin, and I flinch as we both hold ourselves rigid and locked.

The second the last pulse of his cock ends, he wrenches his entire body away from me, pushing off the bed.

It's strange to breathe easy after being constrained for so long. Strange to have nothing on top of me, between my legs. I can't move, though. I'm collapsed on the bed, just wreckage left behind.

His hand is shaking as he runs it over his face.

He gives me one last look. Full of accusations. And longing?

Then he stalks from the room, leaving me behind in a puddle of my own arousal and blood.

CHAPTER SEVENTEEN

I WAKE UP back in my bedroom to the sound of knocking. I only vaguely remember leaving his room and wandering through the third floor. There were so many of them. I actually got lost again, confused about which floor I was on—expecting to circle back to where I started only to discover new rooms. Ivan was nowhere to be seen, so when I found my bedroom again, I took a shower, fingers careful against tender skin, and then climbed into bed.

Voices drift up the stairs, and I force myself to sit. The room spins for only a few minutes, and then I gingerly place my bare feet on the cool wood floor. I find my clothes in the dresser, along with some new things I know I didn't buy—a pink dress with a white pinafore. I finger the silky-smooth fabric, a strange pang of longing in my chest. He must have ordered Luca or someone else to get my clothes from my apartment. That means I won't be returning for a while—probably never.

I'm limping by the time I make it down the stairs. Ivan fucked me with the intent of hurting me, and he succeeded. Through the open door, Blue's low voice confers with Ivan, while Lola shoots questions at them both. *Why didn't you call me when you found her? Was she okay? She might have needed me.*

Bless her.

Somehow she took it into her head that we were friends, years ago. She started caring about me, and then I couldn't help but care back. I tried to be like Ivan, cold and ruthless. At sixteen, cast out and alone, it had seemed like a romantic ideal I could try to reach.

Try and fail, anyway.

I care about Lola. I care about the rest of the girls. I even care about the Grand, which is a *building*.

And most of all I care about Ivan.

Luca is standing in the hallway a few feet away from the entryway. A respectful distance, but one where he can still hear everything. He watches me approach in silence, taking in my limp.

"What a good guard dog," I purr when I get close.

His eyes are hooded. "Did he hurt you?"

He already knows the answer to that. "Why, are you going to defend my honor?"

That earns me a dire look before he stares straight ahead.

The room falls silent as I step into the doorway. I straighten, hoping to hide my soreness. Ivan's gaze finds me first, snapping to me as if he knew I'd been there. He looks like he usually does, rough but well crafted, his tailored suit caressing his powerful body. I would never have imagined those scars underneath, such a smooth veneer covering a rough underground. It mirrors the flash bang of Tanglewood itself, covering up a gritty underworld. Ivan stares at me, and I stare back—both of us reeling, I think, from what we did last night. What we shared. I gave him my virginity and he gave me honesty, but I think his gift was greater.

Lola breaks the silence, rushing across the room and flinging her arms around me. "Oh my God, we were so worried about you. Ivan called us when you went missing."

I aim for a smile. "You know me. I always land on my feet."

The worry in her wide brown eyes doesn't fade in the slightest. "What happened last night?"

My stomach flips. I'm guessing she doesn't know I tried to leave for good. Otherwise she wouldn't be so happy to see me now. Something tells me I won't be able to evade these questions for long. They want answers. Ivan will want answers.

I need to be seated for this. I'm already swaying on my feet.

Lola notices immediately and guides me to the sofa. "Candy. What's wrong? Are you sick?"

I feel a little sick, thinking of telling them the truth. The whole truth. Nothing but the truth. The lingering soreness between my legs doesn't even register in the face of this.

Blue is watching me with a hawklike expression, not missing a thing. I'm guessing he can see how I'm moving stiffly too. And Ivan…is Ivan. Stone-faced. Unreadable.

It's like being in love with a statue.

Blue clears his throat. "Candy, I'm taking this threat against the Grand very seriously. We all are. We're working closely with the police department, but we're also conducting our own investigation." His expression turns wry. "As you can imagine, it would be helpful if we could find him first."

First? If they found whoever did this, the police department never would. They'd just find an anonymous body in the river six months later.

"The blood?" I whisper.

"Sheep's blood," Blue answers grimly.

I should feel relief. At least it wasn't a person who had to die for that. But all I feel is dread, because there are sheep on Harmony Hills. He'd have easy access to it...

Blue comes to sit in the chair near the sofa. Lola is on my side, probably for support. I feel caged in, tensed. There's nowhere to run. I don't imagine Luca would let me leave anyway. "Ivan says you have a guess as to who's doing this," Blue says.

Ivan remains standing, leaning against a hutch, arms crossed. He doesn't move in any way to acknowledge Blue's words. He doesn't even acknowledge me—just stares into my eyes.

I look down. *Shit.*

"Little one," he says softly. I'd know that voice anywhere. I hear it in my dreams.

His cold facade cracks for just a second, letting me

see inside. To how much he needs me to do this. To how much he cares about the Grand and the girls who work there. To how much he trusted me, that he called Blue to get this information from me—even though Ivan doesn't want to believe it's connected to my past. He doesn't love me, and after what I saw of his body last night and how hard he fucked me, I think he even resents me. But he trusted me enough for this.

I take a deep breath. "I think the person doing this…might be from my past. From where I was before I got to the Grand. It's a place called Harmony Hills. From the outside, it's a farming community."

"And from the inside?" Blue prods gently.

Lola hugs my arm tighter, a silent and strong witness.

I close my eyes. "From the inside, it's a religion. Everything, from where you sleep and how much you eat is determined by how…by how sinful you are."

The room has grown deathly quiet, almost as if the house itself is listening. It's that stillness that allows me to go on. "People don't get to leave. It's not a choice. If someone thinks about leaving and people find out, they'll disappear. Not take their stuff and leave, they'll just…disappear."

Lola's face is solemn. "Why didn't they get caught?"

"It's really isolated. Far away from any city and they're mistrusting of outsiders to an extreme. We're told the world is a bed of sin, that the only salvation can be found by turning our backs to it."

Blue raises an eyebrow but doesn't comment on that.

"You think someone from there is doing this?"

"Someone in particular. I mean, I don't know if he's doing it by hand, but nothing happens from the church without Leader Allen ordering it to be done. He's the voice of God."

The silence that follows is thick, and I realize that I didn't qualify my statement. I didn't say he's the voice of God *for those people*. I just said he's the voice of God. My face heats in a blush. "Sixteen years of indoctrination is hard to lose," I say weakly.

Ivan's voice is soft but unmistakable. "How did you get out?"

"My mother. She was—" This will be the hardest part. I can already feel my throat closing up. I clench my hands together. Lola puts her hand on top, warm reassurance. "She was his whore. She had been a prostitute on the outside. When she got pregnant with me, she went to Harmony Hills so that Leader Allen could...could save her soul."

"Why did she send you away?" Blue asks. "Did she grow disillusioned with the teachings?"

"No. I don't think so." I shiver against the ancient shame. Thousands of men have seen my naked body, have lusted after me, but all of that can't erase the filth of Leader Allen's dark lusts. "I think she saw the way he was looking at me."

Lola makes a strangled sound of outrage.

"She didn't even try to go with me. Maybe she believed what Leader Allen said about women being...evil.

About leading men to temptation." My laugh is hollow. "Maybe she wanted to save Leader Allen's soul."

Blue's eyes are shrewd. "Why do you think they're responsible for the messages?"

I meet Ivan's gaze from across the room, and the fury there lends me strength. "That's the stuff he'd always talk about in his sermons, how God had sent down shepherds to guide us. How he had to handle the stray sheep so they wouldn't lead the rest of us to sin. I know it's a common enough theme in religion. It might not be connected to them, but…"

This is where my voice cracks, and I stare at my lap, unable to go on. I've already told them more than I've told anyone. This last part, it will break me.

The sofa cushions shift, and Lola moves away from me. They're leaving, I realize distantly. But then Ivan's hands are lifting me, his arms around me. He pulls me onto his lap, the way I was the night in the dining room. Except I had crawled into his lap that time. This time he put me here—and in front of Lola and Blue too.

I look up at him, and I know the questions are plain in my eyes. His expression is severe but not unkind. "Finish it," he says softly.

He might only be giving me this comfort to get the information out of me. A man like him could be that ruthless. I don't care. I soak up his warmth and his strength, curling myself into a tight ball and pressing harder into him.

"A week before my mother sent me away, Leader Allen called me into his room for private prayers. He had done that before. Usually he talked about my mother, told me she was a sinner, that there was a demon inside her, that we should both pray for her soul so she didn't wind up burning for eternity."

Ivan strokes my hair, almost absently. I'm not sure he knows he's doing it.

"This time...this time was different. He asked me if I was serious about shaking off the shackles of sin, if I was willing to do what it took to fight evil. He said it would be hard and scary, that only a true disciple could survive it."

He did more than just talk to me that day. He touched me, only outside my robes. It was enough. Enough to change the look in his eyes from a suggestion to a promise. And it would have escalated quickly if my mother hadn't sent me away. I always wondered how she knew that it had gotten worse, if somehow she saw him with me that day. That she might have seen us is more shameful to me than the act itself—and for that reason I don't tell Blue and Lola. I don't tell Ivan. They don't need to know about that detail. It would only enrage them, and it wouldn't bring us any closer to finding the culprit.

I open my eyes, startled to meet Blue's gaze. Of the three people in this room, I'm the least close to him. Lola is my best friend, and Ivan is my lover. Even Luca, standing outside the door, is like a brother to me. Though Blue worked at the Grand, we were never close.

I still see murder in his eyes as I describe something I now understand to be a form of grooming. It sickens me, because back then I hadn't seen anything wrong.

All I had wanted to do was please Leader Allen.

The very worst thing is that even though part of me understood the look in his eyes, part of me knew what he would ask of me, I had been willing to give that too. Anything to please him.

Just like my mother had been.

"He said that other people wouldn't understand, that they were not adhering to the word of God. So we could…we could never tell them what we did. I hadn't talked much during these sessions, but I had asked him then, why didn't the sinners outside Harmony Hills read the Bible. He told me that some of them didn't care, that they were disciples of the devil. But he said that some of them, they *did* care, but they were following false prophets, misinterpreting the scriptures."

My hands curl into the soft fabric of Ivan's shirt, needing that anchor. He tightens his hold around me.

"He told me that one day, with my help, the people would find their path to God. He said that's why he needed me so much. He said…he said, 'So there will be one flock, one shepherd.'"

Lola sucks in a breath. "John 10:16."

"And the other one, he didn't quote it exactly, but it would be hard to think of a member of his flock who went more astray than I have." I manage a wry smile. "I kind of made it my life's mission for a while there."

"Find out everything you can," Ivan says to Blue. "I want any information the police have on disappearances or criminal activity. I want financial records. Everything."

Blue nods. "I'll find out if any of his flock have been taking trips recently."

"They won't leave a paper trail. If they've evaded the cops this long, they know how to be careful. Besides, we already know that whoever's fucking with the Grand is good. That's why we haven't found any trace of him."

"What should we do?" Luca asks. "A preemptive strike? Hit them and then they'll know not to fuck with us."

"I have no desire to harm innocent people. And I have no desire to hit a hornet's nest when I have my own snake to deal with at home. No, we find out if they are involved before we move on them."

Luca narrows his eyes. "But if they've covered their tracks that well…"

Ivan's eyes glitter. "I'll find out if they were involved, even if I have to go there myself to do it. And if they are, I'll rip them apart."

Chapter Eighteen

For most of my life I've been torn by guilt. Guilt over the demons inside me. Guilt over my gender, my body, my desire. Being born a girl marked me as evil, according to the teachings of Harmony Hills. Even though I've been gone for years, I've never been able to shake the sense of shame.

I find Ivan in his study. His desk in the Grand is carved wood, contrasting with the stark concrete basement. His desk at home is just the opposite, an industrial construct of slate and steel set in a wood-shelved library. He sits behind the desk, facing the windows behind him.

Dusk creeps over the city, pushing yellow rays through textured windows. From inside you can't see the bulletproof glass that protects you from the outside.

Ivan doesn't look up from the photograph he holds. He doesn't stir when I put a hand on his shoulder. "May I?"

Wordlessly, he holds out the picture. Blurry shapes form a black-and-white panorama. The silhouette of a man is hidden partially by a hood. He's raising something up. A paintbrush? The brick wall behind him glistens with blood.

"Is it him?" Ivan asks.

I study the man, but he's only a shadow here. A suggestion. "I can't tell. I'm sorry."

Ivan just stares at the windows, chin cupped loosely in his hand. "He never looked at the cameras. Never paused or stumbled, even though it was pitch-black in that alley."

A knot forms in my throat as I stare at the shadow. "Leader Allen would have called that divine intervention."

The suggestion of a smile ghosts over Ivan's lips. "I was thinking inside job."

"Oh." Embarrassment washes over me. Of course. That's how ingrained those teachings are, how unshakable their hold. Dismay tightens its band around my chest as I think about what he said. I don't want to imagine anyone at the Grand could have betrayed it. "Who are you thinking of?"

"West is new."

"No. He wouldn't."

One eyebrow rises. "Do you know that for sure?"

I look down. The floor is made of thin wooden planks that form diamond shapes. "Blue trusts him."

"Blue could be involved too."

Worry claws at my throat. "He's with Lola."

A soft laugh. "That doesn't make him innocent."

I can't bear to think Blue is involved, because it would mean Lola isn't safe. As the owner of the security company, he has complete access to the club. None of the girls would be safe. "Don't you trust anyone?"

"No," he says gently. "No one."

And I know he isn't talking about West or Blue. He's telling me that he can't trust me. That he can't be with me, not how I want him to, and my heart gives a hard pang.

"There's something else," he adds. "Bianca never came back to work after her sudden day off."

Dread is a deep well inside me, swallowing me whole. "No. I mean it. *No.* One of the girls would never do this, would never help someone like this."

"Money is a powerful motivator," Ivan says, emotionless. "Especially to a woman in trouble. Or she might not have known she was helping him until it was too late."

I think back to everything I knew about Bianca—and all the girls. I can't believe they would turn against us this way. Not for anything. Leaving is one thing, but putting the rest of us in danger? "She wouldn't have."

"Actually…" Ivan turns his chair to face me. "I don't suspect her. Not that way. I am considering that she might have been the target of this person all along."

Fear makes my heart beat faster. "That would mean she's in trouble."

"It's been over forty-eight hours since she was last seen, Candy. Trouble isn't the word."

The photograph slips from my fingers and floats to the floor. "Stop it. She's not dead."

"Do you want me to lie to you?"

"Yes. No! I want you to stop being this cold, emotionless…" I trail off, not sure what I was going to say.

"Monster?" he asks softly, and I flinch. It's the first reference either of us has made to what happened last night. "What I am can't be changed. Not even for you. But it has its uses. I can consider all the possible suspects without emotion. Whereas you…"

"What about me?"

"You're just a little girl," he says softly.

I lift my chin. "I'm not innocent and I'm not stupid. I know exactly how the world works. I'm a *stripper,* for crying out loud. A slut. A whore. A demon, just like my mother—"

"Quiet," he says, so soft I almost don't hear him. I fall silent immediately, but the tears that stream down my face, they tell the whole story.

The fact that my mother sent me away…I can't help but feel grateful. I know I couldn't have escaped any other way. I can't help but feel angry either, for not coming with me.

For choosing him over me.

"Kneel," Ivan says, and I know then I wasn't wrong. I am like my mother, because Leader Allen told her to kneel and she did. I'm the same, obedient until the end.

At least for one man.

I can feel the wooden slats against my shins. I lower my head, ashamed and somehow aroused. God, was this why my mother did it? Some kind of sick lust? Maybe we do have demons inside us.

The toe of his Italian leather shoe nudges my knee. "Wider," he says.

I spread my knees wider and he leans down to cup my pussy through the jeans. "You're *my* little girl," he says, more seriously than I've seen him say anything. His eyes are piercing, sending some message I can't decipher. It eases something inside me, sloughing off some of the shame, leaving me more naked than before.

"Why?" I whisper.

"Why what?" he asks, his tone patient as he opens the button of my jeans with one hand. His other hand is on my shoulder, brushing his thumb against the pulse in my neck.

"Why do you like me to call you Daddy?"

"Because it makes my cock hard."

That's not the real answer. It might be true, but there's more. "And?"

His hand is warm against my sex, but his gaze—it burns. "Is it so wrong to want to take care of you?"

"No," I say, dropping my gaze. His hand looks large between my legs, claiming ownership, protective and possessive. "But that doesn't mean I have to call you Daddy."

"What should you call me instead? Your boyfriend?"

The word sounds silly when I'm still sore from the way he treated me, my sex throbbing against his palm. It would be far too tame a word to describe him no matter where he touched me. I shake my head.

"Because I want you to trust me," he says softly.

"Trust me to take care of you."

"The way I never trusted… him." Leader Allen. I was once a devoted follower. I would have done anything he asked. But I was always afraid of him.

I'm not afraid of Ivan—not as much as I should be. He's dangerous. Lethal.

"Daddy," I whisper.

"Yes," he says softly. "I like to hear you say it. That's enough reason for me to make you." He pauses before slipping his hand inside my panties.

I flinch, already expecting the worst. My skin is tender where his fingers are, on the outside, but I know it will be worse inside.

"Shh," he soothes. "I was hard on you yesterday. This won't hurt."

It does hurt when he finds my clit, but it feels good too. I spread my legs wider so he can reach me better, and he nods in approval. His fingers toy with my clit, sliding along either side, dipping into my slit to gather wetness.

"Do you know the story of the minotaur?" he asks, his voice conversational.

It's a struggle to focus with his hands playing with my sex. The schoolroom at Harmony Hills had taught us almost nothing. We learned about the Bible, as interpreted by Leader Allen, and how to be good, obedient disciples. Only the boys were taught to read and do math. Girls quit school early, and me even earlier. Everyone knew that my mother was Leader Allen's whore, even if no one said the words out loud. I think everyone knew that I would take her place, too.

I struggle to remember from tutors and textbooks.

"He was…" A gasp interrupts my words as his forefinger slips inside me. "He was half-man. Half-bull. He lived—" Another gasp. "In a maze."

"That's right. And every year the cities would send their young men and women—virgins, naturally—as a feast for the minotaur."

"Until one of the men killed him."

A strange smile twists his lips. "Well, every story needs a hero."

"You're not a monster."

He ignores me, fingering me deeper. "The thing about the minotaur is that he knows what he is. He can't pretend to be a human. He can't pretend to be a bull. He's trapped in that maze, not by the walls outside it, but by what he is."

I grab his forearm, feeling the muscles flex. "You're not a monster, Ivan."

He adds a second finger, and I squirm. His arm on my shoulder holds me down. "There's no use pretending he's something different. He doesn't even want to. But can you imagine how it would feel to find a sacrifice you wanted to be there? Who begged to stay?"

His fingers speed up, and I rock my hips against them, unable to slow down, unable to stop. "You're not—You're not a—"

He pinches my clit, and I soar over the edge, the climax like fierce wind against my face. I close my eyes against the blur and feel tears streak down my cheeks. I fuck his finger, seeking the last breathless rush before I crash at the bottom.

He does up my jeans with deft hands, efficient now.

Wet fingers press into my mouth, and I can only let him in. Only suck to clean him.

"No more questions," he says softly. "I want you to call me Daddy because I want you to know that when we're together, I'm the only one who can tell you what to do. And I will always do what's best for you, even if you don't like it. I will always give you what you need."

I shudder, my insides clenching around nothing as my orgasm gives one final pulse. My eyes are wide, lips stretched around his fingers. I nod yes.

"And you're my little one, because you want to be so good for me, don't you? You want to be taken care of, cherished and punished. Isn't that right?"

He removes his fingers from my mouth and leans back, studying me.

"Why didn't you—"

"What is it?"

I bite my lip. "Why didn't you want me to call you Daddy last night?"

He had put his hand over my mouth and fucked me into the bed.

He's watching me from beneath heavy lids. "I didn't deserve the name last night. I was angry, and I didn't take care of you."

We've been circling each other for years, teasing each other with bad behavior and punishments. The first time he did it, I had already been living in my own apartment and working at the Grand. I'd shown up for work late, and he'd swatted me over my panties. We'd dared a little further each time, but never going all the way—never actual sex until last night. It had left me unfulfilled and a little afraid, for exactly the reason he said.

I dare to put my hand on his leg, right below his knee. "Please, Daddy. Show me what it would be like with you. When you take care of me."

Icy lust flashes through his eyes. "I am taking care of you, little one. That little pussy needs time to heal. I'm sure you're sore today, aren't you?"

A flush heats my cheeks. Very sore. "I don't care about that."

Two hands lift my chin, and I meet his eyes. "I care," he says softly. "I'm not going to fuck you again until you're ready to take me. But if you want to please me…"

My body tightens. "Please."

He cups my cheek. "So pretty. So eager. And such a fuckable little mouth."

The thing I can never tell anyone—not even Ivan—is that I would have done this no matter what. If I had stayed at Harmony Hills, Leader Allen would have used me this way. He'd groomed me for this purpose my entire life, not just at the end, and that grooming made me who I am. A disciple. *A victim.* I'd have been on my knees for him. I'd have been a good girl.

The difference is that I chose this. I chose Ivan. He may be a monster, but he's my monster.

"Take me out," my monster says.

I fumble with his pants. The button and the zipper are like foreign technology, my fingers suddenly clumsy. He is already hard, but I feel him grow thicker as I work him free. It makes me blush, feeling the effects of my awkward obedience.

The suit pants give way to a soft, stretchy boxer material. I glance up to find him staring right at my face. He isn't looking at what I'm doing with my hands. He's studying my reactions, and it makes my heart beat double time. What will he see? Nerves? Excitement?

I don't know what he wants to see.

The skin of his stomach is hot as I slip my fingers under the waistband of his boxers. His abs are hard, and they ripple at my touch. I pull gently, but the fabric is caught against his erection. I'm afraid to pull very hard, afraid of how much pressure is okay. I have some experience with cocks, touching them, rubbing my ass against them in the club, but that knowledge is limited—and it slides away under the role I'm in. The innocent little girl.

He makes no move to help me or to free himself. He just watches me with an intent curiosity to see what I'll do next. What I do is use my other hand to grasp his shaft and carefully pull the fabric over his cock. He feels impossibly hard against my palm, silk smoothed over a steel rod. His cock flexes in my hand, and I jerk back, letting him go with a sound of surprise.

"I'm sorry," I whimper. "It scared me."

"You're doing great, little one," he says soothingly. "You did exactly what I asked you to. Daddy will never get mad at you for that."

Men like to teach you things. That's what gets them off.

"What should I do next?"

The amused light in his eyes says he knows exactly what I'm doing. And that he likes it. "Lift up your shirt. I want to see your pretty nipples."

Instead of obeying him, I cross my hands over my breasts. "What if you don't like them?"

"Why would you think that?" He seems genuinely curious.

He's seen them a hundred times already. And the insecurity is completely real because of it. He's seen them a hundred times and never been overtaken with lust to the point that he had to have me. He's seen me and rejected me. We're playing a game where all of this is new—and it is, in a certain way. But in another way it's the inevitable conclusion to years of foreplay. Both a beginning and an end.

"Because you've seen a lot of girls." It's a form of torture to be this open, this honest, like needles pressing under my nails. These words are everything I've ever feared. "How can I be special?"

He could ruin me with his answer.

He leans forward. "Candace, I'm sure your nipples are as pretty as the rest of you. But they aren't what make you special."

I look down, still cupping my breasts, shielding them. "Why then?"

He reaches out and taps my arms, and I let them fall. He cups my breast gently, his thumb fanning over my nipple. It stands up beneath the tank top. He keeps rubbing back and forth until the twinge between my legs grows sharp.

"Because of how sweet you are," he says softly. "How hard you try to be good for me. Do you know how rare that is? How special? There is no other girl like you, Candace."

"I'm not," I say, and it comes out almost on a sob. "I'm not good. I'm always talking back and not listening and—"

"It's normal for little girls to test their boundaries, to push them. That doesn't make you bad. But you always come back to me, don't you? And you always take your punishment so well. That's what makes you good. That's what makes you special."

But can you imagine how it would feel to find a sacrifice you wanted to be there? Who begged to stay?

I reach inside me to find the strength—and grasp the hem of my tank top. It's a completely different experience than stripping onstage, because I'm a different person. Onstage I'm Candy, the sexy, fearless, powerful woman who knows how to use her sexuality to get everything she wants. In this house, under Ivan's pale gaze, I'm his little one, helpless and hopeful, afraid but eager to try.

He moves back just enough to let me pull off the tank top. My skin pebbles under the cool air. His eyes roam over me as if he's seeing me for the first time. "Perfect," he says, and relief washes through me. My Daddy wouldn't lie to me.

He touches me again, cupping my breast as if I'm precious. It makes me push my shoulders back and thrust my breasts into his touch.

He makes a sound low in his throat. "That's right. And I'm going to look at these while you lick my cock."

I eye the erection jutting up from his pants. "Lick your c-c—"

"My cock," he says patiently. "You see that drop right there on the tip? That means it's ready for you to taste."

"It does?"

"You're going to drink a lot of it," he says, a hint of wryness in his tone. "Good girls always swallow."

"Oh." I lean forward and breathe in the salty musk of him. Both of my hands grasp his cock, as if I'm preparing for something huge—and well, I am. He's a lot bigger than I expected when he's close to my face. The prospect of fitting him in my mouth is daunting. And this is a big step, maybe bigger than when he fucked me into the bed last night. Because this isn't something he's doing to me. It's something we're doing together.

The first taste is sharp and shocking, and I gasp as I swallow down the salty come. He's doing that thing again, where he watches me fumble. I think he likes watching me be awkward and clumsy while I try to please him, fumbling around with more submission than skill.

"Is this right, Daddy?"

"You're doing great. Lick it again."

So I do, licking him again and again until his thighs are rock hard with tension and his cock is streaming precum. I almost can't keep up drinking it. If this is how much he can produce before he comes, I have no idea how I'm going to swallow it all down when he finishes.

"Ahh, that's good. Now suck me, little one. Take me in as far as you can."

It feels natural to slide him between my lips—more natural than licking him, even. I coast along the curved edge marking the head of his cock. My tongue flicks at the slit that produces all that precum for me to drink. I can't go very far, but he doesn't seem to mind—for now.

I wrap my hands around his legs to support myself and give me leverage. His muscles are completely taut underneath my hands, trembling with the strain of...what? Holding back? Or giving in?

His gaze roams over me like a caress, from the crown of my head to my stretched lips to my exposed breasts. My nipples are hard under his gaze and the open air.

"I'm going to finish." His voice sounds rough, almost pained. "You're going to hold my come in your mouth. Don't swallow. And don't let any slip out. Understand?"

I nod without releasing him. It's almost a shock when his hands close behind my head. I jerk away and then catch myself. He doesn't reprimand me, just holds me inexorably while his hips pump faster than I had done for him.

Then his grip tightens even more, and he slides in farther than before.

His cock nudges the back of my throat, and I struggle not to gag, struggle not to fight him as he holds me in place. "Ah fuck," he mutters between clenched teeth. "So fucking good. Hold it. Hold it in."

Hot liquid fills my mouth, almost spilling out of my lips as his cock continues to pump in and out of me. I seal my lips as hard as I can, struggling to keep it in. The urge to swallow it is strong now that my mouth is full. It's *too* full, with his come and his cock still pulsing.

As his climax fades, he relaxes back in his chair. "Perfect," he says, sounding relaxed, almost drugged.

I make an urgent sound, still holding all of him in my mouth.

He looks at me from beneath heavy lashes. His smile is knowing and almost mischievous. "Hold it, girl. Don't make me spank your ass tonight."

The sound I make is pure frustration.

It only seems to please him, and he settles into the chair, leaning back, looking supremely comfortable as his cock softens in my mouth. "I know it's hard," he says, only sounding a little sympathetic. "But I think you can hold it. Just until I'm hard again. Once you have two loads, you can swallow."

I know my eyes must be wide as saucers, because I

can't believe what I'm hearing. Two loads? My lips are already trembling with the effort of holding in one.

He doesn't bother arguing the point. He just sighs with obvious pleasure and caresses the hair at my temple.

The strain of keeping all of it in my mouth, of not being able to swallow, begins to break me apart. It hurts in a way that his rough hands and hard cock couldn't pierce me last night. I feel my will begin to wear down. I didn't even know I'd been holding on to something stubborn, something prideful before this, but I feel it crumble now.

My own body works against me, producing saliva to combat the salty, sticky flavor of him. It only produces more liquid for me to hold. Some of it dribbles out of the side of my mouth. I must look dirty. I must look pathetic.

His expression is nothing short of admiring. "You're beautiful like this," he says softly.

I can only blink up at him in response. My eyes fill with tears—a physical reaction to the stress of holding my mouth like this. And an emotional reaction to the vulnerability of it. I'm subservient to him in a way I had never imagined I could be. And I realize I was wrong before, to compare him to Leader Allen. Leader Allen may have touched my body. He may have made me kneel. But he would never have dominated me like this, so intensely it feels like I'm ripping apart just to please him for one second longer.

My lower lip is trembling now, almost violently with

the effort. I feel the first twitch of his cock, and I realize that it's my strain, my suffering, that's getting him hard again.

The first time he came was a long buildup, steady thrusts and tender touches. This time he starts fucking my mouth almost right away. His hands lock behind my head. Short, fierce thrusts take me by surprise, and I can't keep the come inside anymore. It spills out of my lips and down my chin. I don't have time to wipe it or even feel embarrassed because he's going too fast. I can only kneel with my mouth open as he finishes himself off.

In the end he presses deep—deep enough that swallowing isn't a choice. Thick, hot come pulses at the back of my throat, and I swallow to keep from choking.

He holds me that way, cradling my head until he's finished. When he pulls away, I move to wipe my face, but he stops me with a soft negative sound. "Wait here," he says.

He returns in a minute with a warm washcloth, which he uses on my breasts, where drops dot my skin, and on my chin. He finds a clean corner of the washcloth and presses it into my mouth. "Suck," he says, and I suckle the fabric until warm water trickles down my throat.

Only then can I ask him the question I've been holding in. "Ivan...tell me you weren't serious about visiting Leader Allen."

Okay, so I don't really phrase it like a question. But I

need to hear him say the words. I need him to reassure me that he'll never confront Leader Allen—especially on his home turf.

Surprise flashes over his face, followed by understanding. He crouches down so we're at eye level—almost. "You think he's terrorizing my club. My girls. You have to know I can't let that stand."

"But I thought you said it wasn't him," I say hopefully, knowing it's useless.

His expression conveys disapproval. "And you said it *was* him. The only way we'll know for sure is to find proof. Since whoever this is covered their tracks very well, the second best option is to confront him."

"You can't—" I struggle for how to say this. "You can't go there. You can't trust him. He'll *hurt* you."

That amuses him. "No, little one. That's not how this will go down."

"You don't know him like I do. You don't know what he's capable of. People disappear there. Not just girls like me. Grown men. Strong men, gone without a trace."

His amusement fades. "All the more reason he should be stopped."

That makes me smile a little. "I didn't realize you were a vigilante."

Ivan cups the back of my neck and presses our foreheads together. "He scared you. That's enough reason for me to kill him without any remorse."

I twist my hands together on my knees. "You can't."

130

An eyebrow rises. "No?"

"My mother…she loves him." No, that's not the right word. "She worships him." I may have a fucked-up relationship with her—or no relationship, really. But even so, I don't want to do that to her.

Ivan frowns. "I can't promise what will happen. If it turns out he's responsible…"

"Maybe I could come with you. If there's trouble, I could get her out." The thought of seeing her after all these years makes my heart pound.

"No," he says immediately. "It's too dangerous."

"You just said it would be fine," I protest.

"For me. I'm not afraid of him. I know his kind. I understand him."

"Because you're a monster too?"

"Yes. And because we both wanted the same girl. The difference is, I have her. Parading you in front of him will only make him want to come after you, even if he wasn't the perpetrator before. I can protect you, but I don't need any more religious nut jobs fucking with my club."

Okay, he has a good point. Still… "They won't even let you onto Harmony Hills without permission. Or an escort. There are armed guards at the entry points."

"How is this convincing me to bring you?"

I hesitate, struggling with a truth I didn't want to admit to myself. "And besides, I really would like to see my mother. One last time. Just to make sure she's okay. I always had to resign myself to never seeing her again, because I knew that if I went back, I'd never leave alive. But now…"

His eyes are solemn. "I'll be sure to see her. I'll offer that she can come with me, to visit you if nothing else. But you have to understand, I meant what I said. You won't be coming with me. Until this person is found and dealt with, you won't be leaving at all."

Chapter Nineteen

I'M NOT GOING to make the same mistake twice. This time when I leave, I make sure Ivan is at some important meeting and his guard dog has the night off. There's a guy watching me in the car across the street, but it's easy enough to go through my bedroom routine backlit by the lamp. I know he's watching me, and I give him a little show—it's only shadows, after all.

And I'm not going to do anything as predictable as hitch a ride. No, that was too easy. He found me the first time, and he'd only find me faster the second. Besides, getting out of the city is nearly impossible. I don't want to involve Clara again, especially since he'd look to her first. And half the cab drivers in the city are in Ivan's pocket.

I need to think unconventional. I need to think strategy.

So I sneak to the nearest gas station and put in a call to Fedor Markoff, otherwise known as Ivan's biggest competitor. He runs a series of underground gambling casinos. I met him during my party days—or rather, party nights. He took an interest in me because of my connection to Ivan.

He's a total prick, which means he'll enjoy pulling one over on Ivan.

I have to go through three representatives before I reach him. "Candy! Have you finally decided to dump that miserable bastard and come work for me?"

Yup, total prick. "Actually I was hoping we could do a little business."

He laughs. "And what is it you want?"

"A ride." I manage to project the casual, confident tones that will keep him interested. Desperation would be an instant turnoff. And I am desperate. "A ride on one of your gambling riverboats."

If I can't leave by ground transportation, I'll go by water.

"You've been on the riverboats before, sweet. What's different about now?"

"I want to get dropped off on the other side."

"Ah. And why would I do that?"

"Because you want to fuck with Ivan. He's already dragged me back once. He'll be very pissed once he finds out I've slipped through his fingers."

"You intrigue me. I don't suppose you'll tell me what he's done to anger you?"

He hasn't done anything but be himself. Dominant and remote and just the right touch of humiliating. I find everything about him sexy, but nothing about him warm. "Do we have a deal?"

"Well, now. Perhaps I will be satisfied to know he's lost something important to him, but how will he know that I was the one responsible?"

I have to roll my eyes. "I'm sure you can work it into a conversation. But later. If he finds me, it defeats the purpose—and you *won't* have fucked with him at all."

Fedor is quiet a long moment, and I wonder if he thinks it's too much trouble just to mess with Ivan. Gambling is technically allowed on the river, unlike the underground casinos. But other things happen on the boats—drugs, prostitution. Naturally, there's a stripper pole. So they don't like to dock more than they have to. It leaves them more vulnerable to getting raided.

"The boat called *Divina*. Do you know it?"

"Yes." Everyone knows it. The *Divina* is his flagship riverboat, complete with suite-like guest rooms and gourmet dining. He actually stole the chef from a Michelin-starred restaurant in downtown Tanglewood. And when I say stole, I mean that somewhat literally. The man was deep in gambling debts, and Fedor made it clear how he would pay.

"Be there in thirty minutes, sweet."

I put the pay phone back on the hook, trying to ignore the sick sensation in my gut. Ivan might eventually pull the records for this phone, but by the time he gets this far, I'll be long gone.

No matter how much I want to, I can't pretend I'm happy about that. I want Ivan. I *love* Ivan, but I can't be his little girl forever.

That's all I'll ever be to him. I know that now.

After that blowjob. *Good girls always swallow.*

And after him telling me no to going home again, even just to say goodbye. He'll always see me as someone to be sheltered—and someone to be fucked.

I can't be his whore either, the woman he keeps in a side room, convenient when he wants to fuck. That's all my mother was, and I swore to myself I would never do it. I would rather dance for a hundred men and be my own woman than belong to anyone.

Chapter Twenty

THE THING ABOUT riverboats, especially one as large as the *Divina,* is that they're basically floating buildings. They're huge, so the motion of the water is minimal. There are glamorous rooms for dining and gambling and fucking. And there are back rooms for sleeping it off.

Fedor greets me with a distracted, "There you are. Downstairs, quickly now. We're pushing off soon."

I don't fault him for being distracted. I'm surprised he met me personally at all. Nervousness twists my stomach. Can I trust him? No, that's a silly question. Of course I can't trust him. All I can trust is his animosity toward Ivan, which is all-encompassing and universal. He's always doing things to fuck with Ivan, things like stealing away key employees or encroaching on his turf, and this will be no different.

I get a few strange looks because I'm in street clothes. A pink polka-dot ruffled tank top and cutoff jean shorts. My sandals have rhinestones on them. So I *might* stand out from the glittering jewels and ball gowns. But even if I were dressed right, I have no desire to gamble. I definitely have no desire to strip. In fact the only thing I want...

The only thing I want is Ivan.

That is the sad truth. I pass by a wall made of mirrors and see myself walking by. I look...young. Is that why he calls me his little girl? But I am a woman. I have the breasts and the ass to prove it. And what's more, I know how to use them. No matter what I do it's never enough.

I'll always be a little girl to him.

I cross my arms as if they can be a shield against these people. Against myself. I don't want to see what I look like. I don't want to see how young I look—because I am young, compared to these people. Compared to how I think of myself. I'm nineteen, significantly younger than Ivan. Maybe that's why he doesn't take me seriously. Maybe that's why he can never see me as his equal.

Instead of remaining in the front rooms, I check in with the concierge to claim an empty back room. I can stay here until we reach the other side. I lie down on the bed and drift off to the faint rhythm of the river, dreaming of blood and poles and gray eyes.

A knock at the door startles me awake.

I reach for the door. "Is it time to go—"

My question gets caught in my throat as I look into the gray eyes of my dream.

"Where were you planning on going?" Ivan asks.

Oh shit. "What? How did you...?"

He gives me a dark look, pushing his way into the room and locking the door behind him. I can't help but swallow hard, fear and anticipation warring in my chest.

He found me, again. He's going to *punish* me. God help me, the first feeling I have is relief.

"Fedor wants to *fuck with me*," Ivan bites out, his tone making it clear that Fedor relayed our entire conversation. "But he doesn't want to start a fucking war. He's not stupid. He knows that if he helped you get away, I would never rest until there was nothing left of him."

I shiver at the certainty in his voice. "But…why?"

"Why?" Ivan's laugh is a cold, hard sound. "Fuck if I know why, little girl. You're more trouble than you're worth. Except I can't seem to let you go."

You're more trouble than you're worth. The words bang around in my head, an echo of everything I ever heard as a child. "I want to leave," I say, backing up. "You can't keep me against my will."

His expression is unforgiving. "Watch me."

I close my eyes, feeling hot tears of frustration slide down my cheeks. "Stop it, Ivan."

He crosses to me in long strides, taking me by the back of the neck. His touch is not painful, but it is firm. "I'm not going to stop. Not until you're begging me. Not until you're so wrapped up you never even *think* about leaving me again."

I stare into those pale eyes, wondering at the depth in them. Wondering at the heat.

Before I can figure anything out, he gives me a rough shove toward the bed. "Strip," he says.

This is familiar ground. And so I walk this ground

with a strut, giving him a little show as I tease down the shorts and my lacy tank top. You'd think a man would get bored with having seen my body—any woman's body—so many times. But the repeat customers at the Grand prove otherwise. As do the icy flames in Ivan's eyes.

"On the bed." His voice is guttural now. He's really pissed, and he's going to fuck me to show just how much. I'm a little nervous. After all, I remember from my first time how much it can hurt. But I want this too, because it means he cares. Doesn't it? Or maybe that's just what my mother told herself every time she went to pray.

Subdued, I scoot back on the bed and wait for further instructions.

When he comes close, he puts his hand on the crown of my head. It feels like a benediction, even as I can sense the fury rolling off him in waves. "You keep leaving," he mutters. "What is it you hope to find?"

I know what he wants. He wants me to give him something specific, something material. *Buy me a pony and I'll stay your docile little girl forever.* Except I can't be that docile little girl. And the more he pushes me to stay that way, the more I sink comfortably into the role, the more sure I am that I will have to leave. A man as powerful as Ivan isn't easy to trick, but one of these days he won't be looking—and on that day I'll leave. And I can't deny, as I look into his eyes, that I will forever be sad when he doesn't follow me.

Two fingers tap my thighs. "Open."

I tremble, spreading wide. "What are you going to do?"

Though the answer seems obvious. He's going to fuck me, and it's going to hurt.

And it seems like that's what will happen when he answers, "I'm going to give you what you deserve, little one."

He climbs onto the bed between my thighs. He's still fully clothed, with his dress shirt and jacket—and his pants completely buttoned. Then he bends down and licks my pussy. I almost shoot off the bed in shock. My body was bracing for pain, but it can't handle this pleasure. I would probably roll right off the bed, but Ivan's hands catch me and hold me down.

He licks my clit until I'm panting—and he's panting too. I can feel his hot breaths against my clit between the tender, tortuous licks.

"Ivan," I whimper. "Please."

His eyes meet mine across my body. Then he's—thank God—tearing off his jacket, his shirt. He's undoing his pants. I only have a second to take in his strong body, his terrible scars, and then he's on top of me, inside of me.

His cock doesn't hurt like before. It's still an invasion, a fullness, a stretch. But without that biting, lingering pain. And I realize now that he'd been holding back, to an extent. I realize it because he doesn't hold back now. He pounds into me, fucking me with everything he has.

He's fucking me for *his* pleasure, not mine. I'm not sure how I know that. Something about the rhythm of it. Or maybe the way his eyes are closed, focused on the sensation in his cock instead of how I'm feeling. It makes me hot to think of the pleasure I'm giving him, makes me hot to be used like an object to get him off. My pussy is pulsing with it, but it's not enough to come.

Ivan stiffens, and I know he's coming inside me. His face is beautiful like this, carnal and raw. He looks like an avenging angel, and I push my hips into him, giving him a final squeeze. He gasps and bucks one last time.

Then he pushes off me, rolls over so he's facing away, and pulls up the sheet. "Good night," he says, still breathless.

For a minute I can only lie there, legs still spread, pussy still hot with arousal.

Then I sit up. "*What?*"

He sounds both amused and tired. "Go to sleep, Candy. We're staying the night."

"I don't mind staying the night. I mind…I mind you leaving me like this!"

He looks at me over his shoulder, expression appreciative. "It wouldn't be a punishment if you liked it."

I should be pissed, but instead I just feel desperate and horny and deeply regretful. "Please, Ivan. Please…Daddy. I'm sorry I ran away. I won't do it again."

His eyebrows lower. "Don't lie to me, little one."

I drop my gaze, because we both know I can't promise that. "Please let me come. I…I need to. It hurts in my private place."

"Show me," he says softly.

I put my hand over my pussy and give him my most sorrowful expression. I don't have to fake it at all, because I feel sorrowful. I can't believe I hurt him that way. And I can't believe how turned on it made me to have him use me with no thought to my pleasure.

With a sigh, he sits up and puts a pillow in the middle of the bed. Then he arranges my body, without asking me, so I'm on my hands and knees, the pillow underneath me. For a second I think he's going to fuck me again, from behind this time, and the pillow is for support.

Then he gives me a cruel smile. "You want to come so bad? This is how bad girls come."

I blink at my position. "What…?"

He slaps my ass. "Move your hips. You know how."

The impact of his hand goes straight to my pussy, and I do rock my hips against the pillow. Humiliation burns my cheeks as I realize how I must look, humping a pillow in the bed. The worst part is, I could have just gone to sleep. If I wasn't so turned on by this, I wouldn't have to do it. It's my own desire that has trapped me here, fucking this pillow, struggling to get friction from the soft sheets. I have to press down hard to get enough—hard and fast. My cheeks must be red with how embarrassed I feel, but somehow that only makes me hotter. Ivan watches me struggle with my arousal, with my humiliation, offering nothing more than a small, pleased smile and a stroke of my thigh.

When I come, my pussy feels rubbed raw. It feels less like pleasure and more like an end to the pain.

But something is different, because when I collapse onto the sheets, exhausted and wet, Ivan pulls me against him. He doesn't turn his back on me this time. His arm is supporting my head, and my hand is stroking his chest.

For a few minutes I let myself drowse like this, content despite the indignity of how I came.

Or because of it.

Then the texture of his scars underneath my fingertips becomes too much to ignore. "Who did this to you?" I whisper.

He tenses, and I know I've ruined it. He'll push me away. Maybe he'll even leave the riverboat.

Maybe he'll leave me on it.

Except then he does what I least expect. He answers me. "I lived with my father. My mother was... not in the picture. My father, he wasn't always around either. He left often, for long periods, drinking binges and gambling, shacking up with someone. It was always a relief when he was gone."

My hand tightens into a fist, and I have to force myself to relax, to stroke him again. Ivan has always been like a force of nature to me. The thought of him as a young boy—vulnerable, hurt—makes me want to punch something.

"It was my grandmother who raised me. It was her house we lived in. She did her best, but she had a soft spot for her son." He laughs abruptly. "More like a blind eye."

I flinch.

"When I was eight, he left for the last time. To this day I don't know what happened to him. I'm assuming he died soon after that, because there was no trace."

My heart aches to imagine a young Ivan not knowing where his father was, even after what had been done to him. Love can survive in the darkest, coldest places. I know that as well as anyone.

"I stayed with my grandmother for a while. Her house, the land… it's a beautiful place. Peaceful. But I was wild. Violent. I fought with everyone I met. She was very old, and my presence only made her life harder. I knew that even then, so I came to the city."

"On your own?"

"I was fourteen."

A year younger than I was when I came to Tangle-wood. I'd been a child then, and he'd taken me in. He'd taken care of me. "Who took care of you?" I ask softly.

He shakes his head, impatient. "I knew enough about the foster care system to know I didn't want to be in it. Some people I knew from school were in it, and their stories reminded me of what it had been like before my father left. So I lived on the streets for a while."

I make a rough sound, and he shushes me. "It wasn't

bad. Really, it wasn't. During that time is when I learned how to deal with people from all walks of life. It's when I learned to love this city, for all its darkness."

I kiss one of his scars, closest to me. A low rumble comes from his chest, and it's another minute before he continues.

"I tried to stay away from adults as much as possible, unless they also lived on the streets. But one day I was too cold and too hungry. I had heard about a shelter in a church. I went there because I thought…I thought they might not turn me in to the authorities." Ivan's voice is completely even, almost mechanical, and that's how I know how much this costs him. "And I was right. Father Michael didn't turn me over to the authorities. He kept me there for three years."

In the absolute flatness of that final sentence, I know exactly what happened in those three years. I know exactly how Ivan became the hard man he is today. His father may have left scars on the outside, but someone else left scars on the inside.

And I know that he understands exactly why I had to leave Harmony Hills, more than anyone else ever could. He understands what came after.

We were both born to a different world, one both simple and cruel.

That world spat us out, leaving us to find out own way among the thorns and brush of the city. Ivan had fought with fists and a cold-hearted determination.

I had fought with my body. With sex.

Where does that leave us? Both of us are broken, in our own ways.

Both of us are longing for home.

Chapter Twenty-One

IT'S LIKE BEING locked in a tower. There are no windows in my room, no mirrors. Only a stack of leftover books that I've read a hundred times. Nothing dirty, of course. Ivan would never have allowed that when I was sixteen and living under his roof. He never cleared out this room. I suppose he didn't need the space. Or maybe he always knew I'd end up back here.

At least I have my clothes and things from my apartment. I pick up a lacy thong and eye it critically. So much ribbons and wrappings. I love them. I can't deny that. I love being a present; I loved being unwrapped. By my own hands, though. The men at the club were not allowed to touch. And Ivan... I never convinced him to unwrap me. Not really.

He didn't want to.

It settles over me, half decision, half trance. I take off my tank top and jeans and put on the thong.

Immediately I start to feel like myself again—like Candy.

I add layer after layer, swirling myself in silks. A pink bustier striped with black. A frill of short lace instead of a skirt. I put on makeup next, thick strokes of glitter and gloss. I brush my hair until it shines, pinning it away from my face. Long pink gloves that cover my arms, leaving my pale chest and shoulders bare. Thigh-high stockings that flash a bit of skin.

The final step is a pair of black stilettos.

The tiny mirror in my makeup bag barely lets me see my face, much less my body. I make my way downstairs to the main floor, and then to the basement. The gym is down here—weights and treadmills. There's also a wide-open space with mats for Ivan to practice grappling and fighting with Luca.

And a wall of mirrors on one side. The first glimpse of myself in those mirrors makes my heart skip a beat. I look like a stranger, like someone pretty and confident and sharp. I want to be this woman. Dressing like her doesn't make it true, but it's the closest I can come.

And dressing like her does *something*. Even walking in these shoes changes my gait, my height, the sway of my hips. I feel sexy and powerful, the way I sometimes do onstage. In this basement there is no one to see me, but I still feel sexy and powerful.

Walking is like dancing, when I move slow and sensual. When I cross the floor in long strides, made longer by the four-inch heels. And then I *am* dancing, swaying my body to music that I can only hear in my head.

I swing myself down low and rise back up, letting my chest lead and my ass flex. I sway and kick and rock my body, with no one to impress. It's about being sexy, but not about a man. It's about *feeling* sexy, alone in the room.

Minutes pass. Hours. I'm covered in a sheen of sweat, breathless, exhilarated.

Dancing like this is almost like being free. Almost like being able to leave this house. Almost.

A throat clears, and I wobble on my shoes, barely catching myself from falling. I whirl, half expecting to see Luca. He'd make fun of me or pull my hair, but it's not Luca standing behind me. Ivan leans against the brick interior wall.

My mouth goes dry. He isn't wearing a shirt. The way his arms cross over his chest makes his muscles bulge. And God, those forearms. Blunt strength combined with precision. My gaze takes in the line of pale hair down his taut stomach. Black sweatpants hang low on his hips.

Jesus.

"Were you watching me?" I ask, even though he was. He's not turning away or looking abashed like another man might. He's just looking right at me, a bemused expression on his face.

"What was that?" He doesn't sound accusatory. Just curious.

It takes me a second to realize what he means. "The dancing?"

"It's different."

Different than stripping. Different even than Honor's ballet. A bastardization of both of them—both sexy and elegant, flashy and demure. "It's burlesque. I've been practicing. Do you like it?"

I've been thinking we could start doing it at the Grand. It's more suited to the space anyway. Still sexy. Just a little more…fun.

He is silent a moment. "I need this room."

He doesn't like it. My heart drops, but I try not to let it show. Blowing out a breath, I walk over to him, putting every ounce of sexy into my step. It's strange being with him like this, sweaty and sultry while he is half-naked. Usually he is the one covered up by a suit.

"Maybe I'll watch you," I tell him.

He shakes his head. "Get some rest."

My gaze drops to his chest. It's magnificent…and heartbreaking. Up close I can see the scars again. Old cuts of unknown origin. The burns hurt me the worst. There's a kind of careless malevolence in them, someone who wanted to make him hurt, who knew no one would ever see or ever care.

My finger touches a scar on his abs, and he tenses. *My father left often, for long periods, drinking binges and gambling, shacking up with someone. It was always a relief when he was gone.*

"Do they hurt?" I ask softly.

His voice is cold. "Does it matter?"

More than anything. "If you're hurting, it matters to me."

His eyes lock straight ahead of him. He's looking at someplace above my head. No, he's really looking into the past. So long ago. The scars are faded, but they'll never go away.

"Did you ever see her again?" I ask softly. "Your grandmother?"

"She passed away while I was… A year after I left."

The grief in his voice cuts like raw glass, that while he was enduring unspeakable things, his grandmother died. The jagged edges are sharp with resentment—that she had turned a blind eye to his father's abuse, even that she had been unable to care for the wild boy he became. Resentment and love. Only love can hurt that deeply.

"Did you ever go back to her house?"

His eyes darken. "There's nothing for me there."

Her house, the land… it's a beautiful place. Peaceful.

There's no beauty for him? No peace?

"But—"

"Don't ask me again."

And the way he says it, it feels like a lash. As if there's nothing for him there—or here, standing in front of him. As if my very presence here is an affront to him. No, less than that. An inconvenience. He's punishing me for pushing him too hard, for making him feel too much.

The silence spins out, making the hair on the back of my neck rise. He doesn't want me here. He doesn't trust me. He won't ever love me. My chest squeezes tight.

I step around him.

He grabs my arm. His eyes are still facing straight ahead. "Don't mistake me for one of the girls at the club. I'm not going to tell you how I'm feeling or open my heart. There's nothing left to open."

My breath catches. "Then why don't you let me go?"

His gaze flicks to me, as cold and cutting as a blade. His hand falls, and I immediately miss his bruising grip on my arm. Without another word, I walk up the stairs to the main floor, feeling his gaze on me the whole way.

CHAPTER TWENTY-TWO

IVAN SPENDS MOST of the next day at the Grand. Luca guards me at the house, under strict instructions not to let me out of his sight. I might fuck with him just for fun, but I'm too distracted. Too nervous about what is happening tomorrow. Ivan is getting an update from Blue and the police department on the investigation, but no matter what, Ivan is going to Harmony Hills tomorrow morning. He's still not letting me go with him.

It's the place where I was born. Where I spent the first sixteen years of my life. I'd once been content with never going back, but now that feels impossible. Something is calling me there. And I feel like I could watch over Ivan, protect him—as crazy as that sounds.

He has dealt with a lot of violent assholes over his lifetime, but there's still something different about the self-righteous, religious, violent assholes like Leader Allen.

And most of all, I'd be able to see my mother again.

Would she even want to see me? I already know she wouldn't be proud of me. Maybe she'd feel like her sacrifice was a waste, when she sees what I've become. Maybe it's best that I'm not going back, so she doesn't

154

have to find out.

"Moved," Luca says.

I scrunch my nose at him. "Did not."

"The pink one," he says, sounding smug. "It moved when you touched it with the green one."

I study the colorful pile of sticks, trying to see where I could have messed up. I'd been so careful. Damn his sharp eyes. "You're lying," I say, pointing the thin pink stick at him. "This was nowhere near the green one."

He rolls his eyes. "You always say that."

"Because you're always lying." And because that's kind of the point of the game. If we wanted a game with actual rules, we'd play Scrabble. Bickering is what makes Pick-Up Sticks fun.

"Fine," he says. "Do it over again."

"Fine." I slide the pink one back where I got it from. Of course this moves the sticks around it, but that's okay since I'm putting it back.

Luca studies the position. Then nudges the green stick so it's *on top of* the pink one. "There."

Oh no no no. "Excuse me? No. The green one was not like that when I started."

"Yes, it was." He pauses. "And *that's* why you moved it."

I open my mouth to object but a knock at the door startles us both. Luca has his gun out of its holster in two seconds flat. He shoves me behind the couch with a rough, "Stay here."

My heart pounds as I stare at the carpet, imagining

Luca silently stalking closer to the door and looking out the peephole. Whatever he sees must not have freaked him out too much, because the lock turns. Then the second lock. And *then* the third lock, because Ivan is a paranoid motherfucker.

Then the door opens. "What?" Luca asks, harsh enough that whoever it is stammers.

"Uh...there's a package for a Ms...Candace Rosalie Toussaint. She has to sign for it."

A shiver runs through me. It's been years since I heard that name spoken aloud. And I know neither Luca nor Ivan have ever heard it, because I never told them. I peek around the edge of the sofa to see Luca's body blocking the doorway. I can only see a little of the terrified-looking post-office deliveryman outside.

"I'm Candace," Luca says coldly.

"Uh..." The delivery man fidgets. Facing off with an ex-mob enforcer really isn't part of his job description, but he doesn't look ready to hand over whatever it is.

With a sigh, I stand up. "I'm Candace."

Luca gives me a scathing look but doesn't stop me from meeting them at the door. A quivering deliveryman hands me a black plastic box with a tiny screen. I sign and hand it back. Luca glowers like he might rip the guy's head off for doing his job.

The delivery man can't quite meet my eyes as he holds out a shaking envelope. Luca snatches the envelope from his hand and slams the door in his face.

I reach for it while he's busy with the locks, but he

just holds it higher. "Hey," I say, "That's mine."

He doesn't even acknowledge me while he peers through the peephole, presumably to watch the guy drive away. And he's still holding the envelope up where I can't reach it. What an ass.

I lean against the wall and cross my arms. May as well; there's no way I can get the envelope unless he lets me have it. "You know what we should get? One of those guns that pops out of the wall when someone comes up. Then they'd have ten seconds to make their case before it shoots them."

Luca glares. "Don't think I won't."

"Ugh, it's ridiculous how good of a guard dog you are. Does Ivan give you treats?"

He ignores that. "All I have to do is tell him that you're in danger and he'll pick up this entire house as is and move it to Iceland."

It's a pretty funny mental picture, I have to admit. My lips quirk. "Even people in Iceland are entitled to mail. Can I have my letter now?"

"No." He scowls. "It could be dangerous."

I eye the letter with more doubt than suspicion. It's one of those document mailers made of thin cardboard—and definitely flat. "Is there a bomb in there? Ooh, I know. A rocket launcher."

Luca is over six feet of brawn and tattoos and experienced malevolence. And he sticks his tongue out at me. "I'm calling Ivan. He'll definitely want to open it first."

"What. An. Ass."

He returns to the living room to grab his phone off the floor. The entire time he holds the envelope over his head, knowing I'll go for it if I get the chance.

"It's me," he says, his voice low and serious. "Some kind of letter showed up for Candy. Yeah, she had to sign for it."

He's distracted. *This is my chance.*

I hop onto the sofa arm, and as he's turning around to spot me, I snatch the envelope from his hand. He swears under his breath as he lunges for me. The lamp crashes to the floor, but I'm already halfway up the stairs. Luca turned into my surrogate big brother for the year that I lived here—which means I'm fast on my feet. I bypass my own room, which does *not* have a lock on it, and race to the third floor.

The third floor, which I had always avoided before. Now I know exactly which room is Ivan's, and I know it has a lock. I close myself in and turn the key.

Luca bangs on the door. "Let me in. *Now.*"

"How about no?" Okay, so maybe I'm taunting a little. It's not very often I get to best him.

"This isn't a game. Open the door."

"Of course it's not a game," I call through the door. "I know why you don't want me to open it. But it's my letter, and I'm opening it."

"I will tear down this fucking door," he yells.

"Good luck with that," I mutter. I have no doubt the lock is steel enforced or something equally ridiculous. Ivan would have insisted on that. Luca can probably bust inside, but not before I open this letter.

If it's some creepy note from the person vandalizing the club—or from Leader Allen—I would have shown it to Luca and Ivan. It's not like I want to protect the bastard sending it. But I want the chance to open it myself. I know they'd never let me. They'd open it for me, dissect every part of it, and only give me the information they want me to see. It's what they did about the note on my mirror and the one in blood. I'm tired of being in the dark.

Besides, the letter was addressed to *me.* Candace Rosalie Toussaint. I have lived for years as Candy, just one name, a bastardization of the one my mother gave me. To hear my real name, to see it in typed letters...I can't ignore the siren call even if it brings me to my death.

There's a little tab meant to tear open the envelope. I do so and then take a deep breath. Inside is a single type-written sheet of paper and a smaller, regular-sized envelope.

I look at the typed paper first. It's on some kind of stationery for a lawyer. It looks very official, but I've never heard of them. And then I begin to read...

...your mother's lawyer and the executor of her estate...

...all funds donated to the Church of Harmony Hills...

...she entrusted me with this letter to her only child

in the event of her death…

The room had seemed so big before, but it's closing in on me. I can't seem to get any air. My hands are trembling as I pick up the envelope.

This one also has the law firm's name and address in the return label—as if she wrote the note in the office. My full name is scrawled across the front. *Candace Rosalia Toussaint.* I didn't see her write that much. There wasn't exactly a stash of paper and pens in our room. That was reserved for Leader Allen and the elders and the boys in school. I still recognize her handwriting, though. I could never forget. She drew the letters into the dirt when she first taught me to read—or tried. Without any books or practice it never went very far.

Only here, with Ivan, have I learned to understand.

Dear Candace,

If you're reading this, it means my time as a sinner has come to an end. Don't be sad for me, because it means I am at peace. I don't know if this letter will find you or if you will want to read it. Of all the sins I committed in my life, what I did to you is the most unforgivable.

If it is any consolation, I brought you to Harmony Hills believing it was for your own good— that sunshine and grass would do for you what streetlamps and sidewalks had not done for me. I discovered too late that it's not the bars that make a jail, but the jailor. And wherever the Good Lord

*sees fit to send me, I will be at peace because I know
that you are free.*

Her name is signed at the bottom: *Rosalie Toussaint.*

I slide to the floor, the letter half crumpling in my
hand. I can't take in a full breath, can't do anything but
shake in the middle of the floor, my knees pulled to my
chest. Tears make the room blurry, and that's a relief. I
don't want to see anything. Not even Ivan's bed and his
big sparse room—normally a comfort. Now it just
reminds me of how much I've lost.

That's how Luca finds me when he finally busts the
door open. I hear wood splinter behind me, but I can't
move. I don't care. At least he doesn't try to touch me,
either in comfort or anger.

It's Ivan who does that, when he gets home a few
minutes later. Ivan who rips the letter from my hand to
read what I could never say aloud. Ivan who drops to his
knees next to me to cradle me close.

CHAPTER TWENTY-THREE

I THINK I might black out for a few minutes. Or maybe longer than a few. The sun has set by the time I come awake in Ivan's arms in the middle of the bed.

"I'll leave tomorrow morning," Ivan is telling Luca, who goes to make arrangements.

"Where?" I mumble. I shouldn't need him. I *can't* need him. After reading my mother's letter, I know that I was right to try to leave here, leave him. But the thought of being away from him right now feels like knives in my skin.

Ivan just gives a short shake of his head, eyes strangely dark. They're usually a pale gray, like an iceberg floating in the middle of the ocean.

Right now they seem dark, like deep waters.

"Don't leave," I whisper. If he leaves now, I'll have to find a way to leave too. I'd never see him again, and I can't bear that thought. Not when I'm so raw.

"I have to go." He presses his mouth to my forehead in a soundless kiss. "This letter proves that someone in Harmony Hills *does* know where you are. Which makes it a lot more likely that this—" He pauses, and my mind fills in the blank with what he'd say. *Fuckhead. Religious nut job.* "That this person is involved," he finishes quietly.

"I'm coming with you."

"Absolutely not. We've discussed this."

"Ivan, I...I *need* to go. I wasn't there for her when she was alive, and now she's—" My voice breaks, and I force myself to go on. "This is the least I can do for her."

His eyes turn to ice. "It won't bring her back."

My breath shudders in my chest. "I know that."

It's the only kind of closure I'll be able to find. They would have already had the funeral, if the lawyer is just now sending me a letter. Funerals happen quickly at Harmony Hills. I have no idea how she managed to even see a lawyer and get that letter stowed away for me, but that won't change anything. I won't ever see her plain wood casket or her unmarked grave. All I'll ever see is that house, without her in it.

It's the only way I can believe that she's gone. Why doesn't he understand?

My voice is just a whisper. "I can't be like you, cutting out the past because it hurts."

"Is that what you think I'm doing?" That mocking voice again.

I know it is. "Then why didn't you ever go back to your grandmother's house?"

"That was a different life," he says, sounding more tired than anything. "Made for a little boy. Not a shell of a man. I'll never go back there. I can't."

I stare at him, realizing he means it.

He picks up the letter and reads it again, his expression severe.

From here I can see something scribbled on the back, something I didn't see before. I take the sheet from his hands gently and tilt it, reading aloud.

And you will know the truth, and the truth will set you free. John 8:32.

Ivan's eyebrows rise. "Even I've heard of that one."

"Why is it on the back like this? It's in her handwriting."

Ivan just strokes my hair, content to let me fall apart in his arms. I push myself up so I'm sitting on my own. "I'm serious," I tell him. "I need to go there and see for myself. That's what she's telling me. The truth will set me free."

He looks dubious, and okay, I admit the logic is fuzzy. But the pieces are there. I can't ignore them. Her writing that Bible verse, scribbled on the back—like an afterthought. But why did she have it? And how did she die? The letter from the lawyer didn't say. She wouldn't be the first person to go missing from Harmony Hills under mysterious circumstances. Of course I won't find out the truth just from looking at an empty room, but I can't ignore her. I can't ignore her final plea.

I clasp Ivan's hands in mine. "Please, take me with you. I *need* to go."

He frowns. "Why do I get the impression that if I say no, you'll find some other way to go."

My head lowers, eyes closed. This is the closest I can

come to prayer anymore. "I left her in that place, in that *hell,* for years. I thought she wanted to be there. I thought she chose to stay."

I always thought she picked Leader Allen over me. After all, she could have gone with me. Or she could have made plans to meet up with me later. She hadn't.

Leave, Candace. Leave and don't ever look back.

Ivan's voice is softer than before, his voice almost gentle. "She's gone, Candace."

"I know that," I say, broken but determined. "But I have to go there, to see for myself. I have to…pay my respects."

She told me never to look back, but this letter is a window to a past I never saw clearly. I could only see her actions as a scared, hurt sixteen-year-old girl. Now I have to wonder what else was happening…

I lean down over Ivan's hands and kiss his knuckles. It's a sign of devotion, a sign of his dominance. His hands tighten around mine briefly before he releases me.

"We leave early in the morning," he says.

Relief fills me. It's clear he isn't happy with me, but he's letting me come.

Ivan closes his eyes and swears under his breath. "One condition. You will not interfere while we're there. It will be dangerous, even with protection. You will not speak. Understand?"

"Thank you," I whisper

He moves to stand. "I have a lot to prepare before then. You should rest. Not here."

Then he's lifting me, carrying me over the carnage of the broken door and down the stairs. He lays me in the middle of my old bed. My eyes are half-closed as I sink into the pillow. He pulls the sheet up and tucks it around me. I'm already drifting as he flicks off the light and closes the door behind him.

Exhaustion has its claws in me, making it hard to keep my eyes open—and ironically, making it hard to sleep. My thoughts are stuck on a wheel, spinning endlessly.

My mother sacrificed everything so that I could live a normal life. And what do I do with it?

Ivan. The Grand. A life of sin.

I didn't have much choice as a naive sixteen-year-old with twenty dollars to my name. It was inevitable that I would have had to sell myself in some form or another to survive. Ivan spared me from the worst of it, feeding and clothing me first, and then giving me safe haven at the Grand.

Now I'm grown and under his roof once again. He puts me on my knees and spanks me. Even when I lived alone, he watched me constantly.

I discovered too late that it's not the bars that make a jail, but the jailor.

My mother sacrificed everything so I could be free.

The only way to do that is to leave Ivan for good.

CHAPTER TWENTY-FOUR

W E TAKE IVAN'S private jet, which is good since I still don't have any identification. Ivan and I don't speak much, but then we're surrounded by his entourage. And by entourage, I mean small army. A set of three black cars are waiting for us. Ivan opens the door to the middle car and waits for me to get in. Surrounded at the front and the back. Protected.

We're as safe as we ever can be, but I can't shake the feeling of dread as we leave the small airport and head toward Harmony Hills. I'm going to see Leader Allen again.

He should be *nothing* to me, but I'm afraid of him nonetheless.

I always knew my mother sent me away to protect me, but I never really knew why she stayed behind. Because she thought it would buy me time? She must have known how unprepared I was, how little I had with me. She must have known what I would have to do to survive.

Or maybe she did love Leader Allen, even knowing what he was. It's a strange feeling, to love your jailor. One I couldn't have understood if I'd never met Ivan.

His expression gives nothing away, focused and completely remote. The man who held me as I cried for the loss of my mother is nowhere to be seen. This is the Ivan who commands respect in all of Tanglewood, the one who made a group of men back off with just a look all those years ago.

"How are you going to get in?" There are gates and locks and guards. We won't be able to waltz in.

Ivan doesn't look at me. "I have an engraved invitation."

Then again, maybe we will. Nervous energy pushes me to keep going. "He won't like you coming here. Even protected, he might fuck with you just because."

"A lot of people have messed with me just because, Candy."

"And what? You kill them? Well, you can't."

"Give me one good reason I shouldn't kill him."

"Because you're coming here in a…in a goddamn parade! They'll know it was you."

The expression on his face tells me he isn't impressed with my reason. "He's a prick."

Prick is an understatement. He's a genuinely horrible human being. I can't really argue with the fact that he deserves to be dead. After the way he treated my mother, and me, and countless other people at Harmony Hills… he's like a dictator. And not the benevolent kind.

Except the thought of seeing him hurt sends ice through my veins. Before I would have said it's because my mother cares about him, but now that can't be my reason. So I have to concede that…I care about him. Not really. Not where it counts. My brain knows I don't care about him, that he's nothing. Less than nothing. But there's a muscle memory in my heart, an old lesson drilled into me, never to be forgotten.

And I hate that. I hate the way he managed to condition me. I hate the way Ivan conditions me. "You just can't, okay? You can't kill someone because they're a prick. What kind of logic is that?"

He gives me a warning look.

Which naturally I ignore. "And you can't just…you can't just *keep* people because you want to. We aren't animals."

"Do you really want to do this now?" he asks, even though he clearly thinks he knows the answer. Of course he thinks that.

And fuck, he's right. I don't want to do this now, but I want to think about where we're going even less. I want to think about my mother and what she sacrificed, what she *lost,* even less. "You don't control me," I tell him.

Then the worst thing happens. He smiles, a little wry. Definitely amused. "Believe me, Candy, I know that. I think everyone who's ever met you knows that."

Now he's just patronizing me. Everyone who's ever met me knows exactly the opposite. Even Lola assumed I was fucking the boss until I told her otherwise. "You know what, Ivan? You can kiss my ass."

"Maybe I will."

God. Everything is so fucking easy for him.

Except one thing. "Excuse me if I'm a little stressed out," I tell him, using the words like venom. "I'm going back to where I grew up, to the place I never thought I'd see again. But then maybe you don't know what that's like."

He goes deathly still.

Like I'm on a suicide mission, I finish roughly, "You're the one too afraid to go home."

His amusement evaporates. "Is that so?"

I'm practically shaking. It's too much. My mother's death. Seeing Leader Allen again. Coming back to the place of my birth, my home for the first sixteen years of my life. "Enough with the fucking rhetorical questions. Yes, that *is* so. You act all tough and fearless, but inside you're just as scared as me. And if you think I'm going to let you *spank* me because I'm telling you the truth, then I suggest you go ahead and try!"

Immediately I realize that the divider separating the front and back is down. Which means Luca and the other guard in front can hear what we're saying. *Shit.*

Ivan looks furious, and I half expect him to accept my challenge. He'll try to spank me, I'll fight him—and he'll win. Of course he'll win. Then I'll be spanked in the back of the limo, with an audience. I'll show up at Harmony Hills with my ass red and my eyes puffy from crying.

It would almost be a relief to cry right now, to be *able* to cry. I want that, but I don't want to show up in front of Leader Allen with that kind of weakness. It would only make him more likely to pounce.

Ivan leans forward. His voice is low, but I have no doubt he can still be heard over the gentle whoosh of the air-conditioning. "If we were at home I would put you in a diaper since you insist on acting like a baby. But since we're not, you can sit on the floor."

I hiss at him, shocked and weirdly turned on by his threat. Even in the midst of a tantrum, I know it isn't the way to convince him I'm grown up. "Excuse me?"

"You heard me. Now, Candy."

I stare at the carpeted floor. It's probably just as comfortable as the seats. And definitely more comfortable than a concrete corner in the basement of the Grand. But still. It's the principle of the thing.

"It's not safe."

His gaze flickers over me. "Because there's no seat belt?"

Of course he's already seen that I'm not wearing a seatbelt. "I'm not doing it."

I expect Ivan to grow enraged at my response, but instead it seems to relax him. So it's a surprise when his fist closes in my hair. He barely has to move his body. Just a twist of his wrist has me sliding off the seat, legs folding underneath me as he forces me to the floor.

He doesn't release me. His hand remains there, tight in my hair, fist against my scalp.

I close my eyes, relieved. When I'm like this, I can breathe again.

When he's holding me, I can be still.

We remain like that over the many miles of the country road. I drift off—not quite in sleep, but not quite awake. It's some floaty place where I don't have to worry anymore. And Ivan holds me tight the whole time, not letting go even when it becomes clear I won't fight him anymore, when someone else's arm might get tired.

Even as a calm settles over me, I hate myself a little bit more. Hate myself for wanting his tender form of captivity, hate myself for needing it.

You don't need it, Candace. The truth will set you free.

"A lot of people depend on him," I say softly. "You may not understand it. Hell, I don't even understand it completely. But there are innocent people there, children too, who depend on him."

Ivan says nothing, staring out the window while holding me in place.

✧   ✧   ✧

WE TURN A corner, and I feel Ivan's body tense. He releases me, and I know we've arrived.

I scramble back onto the seat.

The entrance to Harmony Hills is unassuming, a simple metal arch topped with a metal medallion of the sun coming over the hills. There is no sign and definitely no phone number. There is a gate, but that's not all that keeps people out.

The ground has spikes facing toward the road.

We pull to a stop along the side of the thin dirt road, where gravel fades into grass. Luca steps out of the car to open the door. Ivan steps out first, then extends his hand to me. *Okay then.*

There's a small intercom jutting up from the road that I didn't see before. The black metal box looks like it was installed decades ago, and I'm not sure it's even functional—until Ivan presses the button.

A crackly voice comes across. "Who is it?"

Ivan says nothing, just watches me. Nerves tighten around my throat. My wild gaze catches Luca, who mouths *They can see us.*

I'm the engraved invitation.

I step forward and say in a tremulous voice, "It's Candy." A flush rises through my whole body—heating my chest, my neck. My cheeks. I don't know where cameras would be located, but I'm hoping they're black-and-white. "Candace Rosalie Toussaint."

There's a flicker of static, as if maybe a single short word was said, or maybe the connection was closed. The gate doesn't move and the spikes don't lower, but Ivan tilts his head toward the car. I follow him—taking his lead not to speak unless needed. He seems colder than ever, removed from the rest of us. This is how he's able to do it. How he's able to kill without remorse. How he's able to rule. By being separate. Above us. It's like he told me—he's not so different from Leader Allen that way.

We sit in the back of the limo with cool air and smooth leather for ten minutes.

Then the gate rattles open on its own, remotely connected just like that intercom. The spikes lower. All three cars move forward, down the bumpy road that will take me home.

The road goes from bad to worse, and the limos are forced to stop.

Wordlessly, Ivan steps out and holds the door open for me. We'll have to continue the rest of the way on foot.

I point to the tall house at the end of the lane. "There."

The corner of Ivan's lips lift. "I assumed as much."

Of course, it's the biggest structure here. It's also the only one with regular running water and electricity that doesn't black out at eight p.m. We have to pass all the other houses to get there. Some of them are barely held together, leaning to the side. Some of them are real houses. Where you live is based on how sinful you are. In other words, how much you obey Leader Allen.

I can feel eyes on me as we walk down the bumpy lane. It's tricky to navigate even by foot, rough holes made by rain and loose rocks to remind us where we stand. My heart pounds as I see a curtain twitch in a window.

In the darkness of another house, I can see the whites of someone's eyes as they watch us. In another one, I see the glint of something metal in the window. My heart starts to pound. A gun?

The sun ducks behind the clouds, casting a shadow over the cluster of buildings.

We pass the building that I know is the school, but

there's not a sound coming from it. No crying, no teaching. No slapping. Nothing I could recognize. We might as well be walking through a ghost town except for the smoke that rises from some of the chimneys, preparing for dinner.

We come to a stop at the end of the lane.

"Reverence Hall," I manage to say past the lump in my throat.

That's a fancy name that means Leader Allen's house. It's the nicest one on Harmony Hills, naturally, with central air and real floors. I think the word *reverence* is supposed to be about revering God, but I'm not sure if I ever believed that, even when I lived here. It's about revering Leader Allen, who has so much more than his followers. His wealth is a sign that he lives without sin, which is kind of ironic, since Ivan's wealth means the opposite.

I want to take Ivan's hand. I'm shaking at the thought of entering this house again. Of being that girl again. His posture doesn't invite me to touch him. And he made me promise not to talk once we got inside. He's completely remote from me—part businessman, part criminal. Part avenging angel on behalf of the Grand.

Ivan nods, and Luca steps forward and knocks.

The door opens.

CHAPTER TWENTY-FIVE

S ARAH ELIZABETH IS a year younger than me—I remember her from the schoolroom—but her face is drawn and her doe-like eyes hold an infinite sadness. She looks like she's seen too much, a lifetime of awful things, even though I know she wouldn't be allowed to leave Harmony Hills. She's only seen the same buildings, the same people, who have always been here. I'm the one who's been into the world, who's seen the darker, seedy side of humanity, but I feel almost like Pippi Longstocking next to her.

She frowns at me, surprise and dismay warring in her face, and frowns even more at Ivan.

As soon as she sees Luca, her eyes widen. When she notices his holster, which he isn't making any effort to hide, along with a sinister-looking silver briefcase, she shuts down completely. Any thought or feeling vanishes from her expression, leaving only the glassy-eyed stare of a doll.

"This way," she says, barely a whisper.

She turns away, shoulders hunched under her beige shift.

Ivan and Luca exchange a look. I can read their opinion loud and clear—they think it's fucked up, how docile she is, how blank. Well, so do I. Sarah Elizabeth might even agree.

They don't understand. They can't understand what it's like to grow up with Leader Allen's presence, with his judgment, with his touch.

We follow Sarah Elizabeth deep into the house.

Leader Allen is already seated behind his desk when we arrive. Sarah Elizabeth stands just beside the door, *outside* the room, and I know that is no mistake. She isn't allowed in without his express permission. Even when she is serving him, she cannot presume to enter his presence.

Ivan, of course, presumes. He strides inside the large room as if he owns it. His clinical gaze takes in the old volumes and yellowed pages—and dismisses them just as quickly.

For his part, Leader Allen looks shrewd and wary— and very, very old. I hadn't realized quite how old he was. Or maybe I had, but in my mind that lent him authority. Now he looks the kind of old that's tired, close to death but fighting it every step of the way. His hair has gone from peppered brown to gray. His skin is faintly discolored in places, stretched grotesquely in others. Only his eyes are exactly how I remember them, cunning and cruel.

He doesn't stand when we enter. I suppose that's a show of power, telling us we don't deserve respect. He doesn't look particularly afraid, either, even though Ivan and Luca make an imposing pair.

"I suppose you know who I am," Ivan says in a businesslike tone. "If Rosalie Toussaint's lawyer knew where to find her daughter, then you do too. And you know who she works for."

Leader Allen's gaze snaps to me, and his lip curls. "I always knew you had the devil in you, girl."

Ivan gestures to Luca, who sets down the briefcase with a loud *thunk*. It hadn't seemed heavy when he carried it, but there's clearly something substantial in it. What are they bringing him? Money? No, Ivan would never cave that quickly. And besides, even large stacks of cash wouldn't be that heavy. Guns? I'm not sure how heavy they would be, but Ivan would be more likely to point one at Leader Allen than show him one in a suitcase.

"You don't speak to her," Ivan says softly. "She is not yours. She will never be yours."

Leader Allen's eyes widen in rage, and I think he's about to stand up. But then he settles back in his chair with a leer for me. "Why?" he says, clearly speaking to Ivan. "You've had her for three years. Surely you're tired of her now."

My own anger starts to churn. Of course he's assuming that Ivan has been fucking me all along. He assumes that because *he* wanted to fuck me. And the idea that I would return here, ever, even if Ivan didn't want me anymore... Oh, hell no.

I open my mouth to say something—but Ivan puts

up his hand, stopping me.

Years have passed. I'm not a child anymore; I'm a grown woman. But I'm still listening to men boss me around. My face burns. *He doesn't own me. And neither do you.*

To disobey him, to disrespect him that way, would put him at a disadvantage to Leader Allen. That's the only reason I don't say anything. At least, that's what I tell myself.

Ivan taps the suitcase with one finger, almost thoughtful. "You understand that me coming here, it's a sign of good faith. I could have sent someone. They would have made my point very clear."

Leader Allen leans forward, his face twisted in anger. "This is holy land. God would never let you harm this place."

"He told you that, did he? Well, as it turns out, I have no intention of harming this place. I'm a reasonable man, and there are women and children here." He pauses. "I don't like when women are threatened, you understand."

Leader Allen smiles at me, and my heart drops. "I would never harm a woman," he says. "For they are my flock, and under my protection. But a demon, a demon needs to be driven out."

"Does it?" Ivan says mildly.

Leader Allen doesn't know him well enough to recognize the threat in his voice, but I do.

Ivan flicks the lock on the suitcase and steps back.

Luca does the same, and without knowing why, I step back too. In a smooth motion Ivan opens the lid, and blood comes spilling out of it. But not the pristine smooth red from before. This blood has turned blackish. It's mixed with gravel and brick and coagulated lumps, a horrifying mixture that spills out onto Leader Allen's wooden desk.

He pushes back his chair with a rough sound. I'm surprised he doesn't stand up. Blood spills over the desk but manages to miss his white robes.

Ivan circles the desk slowly, a predator toying with his prey. "How did she pass, *Allen?*"

The way he says Leader Allen's name is mockingly casual, as if they're two friends instead of enemies.

Leader Allen makes a hacking sound. I can't tell whether it's involuntary or a sign of his derision. "Her sins finally caught up to her. I tried to save her—"

"I bet you did," Ivan mutters, looking down with a cold expression. In one move he pulls the back of the chair up, and Leader Allen sprawls on the floor.

Fear flashes across Leader Allen's face, although he tries to mask it. He's collapsed, feet slipping uselessly against the whitewashed floors. Then his expression turns hard, a gleaming light in his rheumy eyes. "I don't have much time left anyway. Pancreatic cancer. If you kill me, it will only make me a martyr."

"Maybe you don't care about your own life," Ivan says, "but I'm sure you care about your flock."

Leader Allen laughs. "Take them then. Kill them.

Fuck them."

I hear a small gasp from behind me, and faintly, I realize that Sarah Elizabeth is still outside the door.

Ivan seems to consider this. Even from across the room, I can see when he comes to the conclusion that Leader Allen is telling the truth—that he's dying soon. That he doesn't care about the people here. Which means Ivan doesn't have any leverage for making him stop.

The decision comes to him suddenly, swiftly. He pulls his gun from the holster, and I gasp.

"No," I whisper. I promised not to speak, but I can't stand here and watch this. "He...he couldn't have. Look at him. He can't get up."

"Then he sent someone." Ivan's expression doesn't soften. If anything, he seems to grow right in front of my eyes. I always thought Leader Allen was godlike, but Ivan looks terrifying and all-powerful. "I don't give a fuck how he managed to do it. In fact I don't really care if he did. He hurt you. That's more than enough reason to kill him."

Something inside me withers at his words. I told him that Leader Allen looked at me, spoke inappropriate words to me, *groomed* me, but I never told him he touched me too.

I never wanted him to know.

The knot in my throat makes it hard to speak. "How did you—"

"I suspected when you first told me what happened. I

knew for sure when I saw the way he looks at you. And the way you look at him."

My gaze snaps to Leader Allen. How am I looking at him? With disgust? With fear? Both of those, but I suspect there's something else in my eyes. Something that Ivan knows very well—worship. The lessons were too well taught, too deeply carved in my soul to be completely forgotten. Even if I've learned to hate him, there's a part of me that will always revere him.

The sound of a gun being cocked slices through me. It's not Ivan's gun. It came from behind me.

I whirl to see Sarah Elizabeth holding a rifle. My heart nearly stops. She's pointing it toward Ivan. I didn't think she had it in her—didn't think she would even know how to use a rifle—but then maybe protecting her leader has given her courage. I'm not sure if she'll hit him. A gun like that will have a big kick, and she looks too thin, too waiflike to even hold it up. But I can't take the risk.

I'm the closest to her, only a couple feet away, and I calmly step in front of the rifle. "You don't want to do this," I tell her softly. "He's not your enemy."

Her eyes are wild, pupils so large I wonder if she's on something. Even though that's impossible. Drugs are for the outside world, not the purity of the hills. "I have to. This is my only chance. Move out of the way."

She steps to the side to get a better shot—and that's when I realize she isn't pointing it at Ivan. She's pointing it at Leader Allen. Oh God, suddenly it's clear to me what Sarah Elizabeth is doing in this house. It's clear who has had to take my mother's place, since I wasn't here to do it. My stomach rolls over.

"Sarah Elizabeth," I whisper. "Don't." Not because I don't want him dead. Whatever I'd felt for Leader Allen, lingering devotion or maybe just pity—it's evaporated now, seeing the fear in this young woman's eyes.

No, I don't want her to shoot because she shouldn't have to. It's an act that would haunt her forever, even if Leader Allen deserves it. I know, because it would haunt me too. Our teachings run too deep. Ivan can shoot him. Or Luca. Hell, I'll do it if it means sparing her one more second of pain, pain that should have been mine all along.

I push the barrel of the rifle aside so it's pointing at the wall. Sarah Elizabeth's eyes are wide, lower lip trembling.

A choked sound comes from behind me, and I turn in time to see Leader Allen stagger to his feet, clearly unbalanced but surging forward just the same. "That's right, girl," he says with a cold smile directed straight at me. "You wouldn't kill your father, would you?"

I freeze in horror, every muscle seized tight. He doesn't mean *father* like a priest. That isn't what we ever called him. He was our leader. Leader Allen. And he's my father... The memory of what he did to me, *of his hands on me,* sears my skin like a brand I'll never be able to erase.

My gaze clashes with Ivan's. In those pale gray eyes I

see my anguish, my horror reflected back at me—along with something I'm too broken to feel in this moment. Rage.

Sarah Elizabeth moves from behind me, pushing forward.

Then Luca is there, holding her back. I hear a scuffling sound and shouting—then a gun goes off. I'm too frozen to move. Too shocked to even care if it's gone through me. I can only stare in horror and fascination as Ivan pulls Leader Allen close and pumps three bullets into his stomach.

The older man slumps to the floor, already unconscious.

Already dead before his body collapses in a graceless heap.

My hands clap over my mouth, barely holding it in. Then I'm running, stumbling down the steps, racing out the door. I make it to the honeysuckle plants outside before I throw up, kneeling in the dirt as my body rejects anything and everything. I'm sick to my stomach, sick to my soul.

My mother knew. She must have known who he was to me. That must have been why she went with him. Even with his precious Harmony Hills, he'd found a young prostitute to fuck in the city. And when he'd knocked her up, he'd brought her and her small child to keep in his house—not as part of his family. As pretty little playthings.

My stomach heaves again, and I lean over the dirt,

mouth open in shock and horror, but nothing is left inside me. I left them in that room. Ivan, Luca, Sarah Elizabeth. The dead body of Leader Allen. I can't bring myself to think of him as my father.

Luca exits the house first, dragging a shrieking Sarah Elizabeth in his arms.

There's blood seeping from his shirt, and I realize he's been shot. It doesn't seem to slow him down any or interfere with his strength. Sarah Elizabeth is fighting him off, but she's losing. Even shot, he's a powerful force. Why is he taking her? *Where* is he taking her? The questions float away, lost in the storm of my hatred, of my shame.

Ivan comes out next. He comes straight to me and helps me stand. He doesn't say a word as we head back down the lane.

The first shot hits the dirt.

It takes me a second to realize what's happening. Ivan realizes it sooner. He swings me into his arms as the second shot rings out and hits the ground, sending more dirt into the air. *Oh God.*

Luca still has Sarah Elizabeth with him, and the men from the other limos circle us, shooting back at the houses.

"No," I scream. "There's children."

The worst part is those children might have guns. The women might too. They're too brainwashed to do anything else. We're demons, come to slay their mighty leader.

"Don't shoot," Ivan tells them as we reach the limos.

The men look angry but they shove us inside, and soon enough we're heading back out.

The gate is closed when we make it back through—but the spikes are facing away from us, meant to keep cars out, not in. The first limo blasts through the gate at top speed. The next limo has Luca and Sarah Elizabeth, though I can't see them. Ivan and I are in the last one.

We tear over the country roads for hours. For eternity.

Ivan confers with his men over the phone.

"No one's hit," they tell him. "Except Luca."

My eyes shut tight against what I saw in that house, what I learned. I curl into a ball.

Only Ivan's touch can calm me now. He's the eye of this storm, the only thing that isn't spinning and destructive in this whole mad place. We drive out of Harmony Hills much quicker than we came, while I shiver uncontrollably, held tight in Ivan's lap.

CHAPTER TWENTY-SIX

I'M LYING IN the bedroom of a penthouse suite in the closest city to Harmony Hills, the same city where the social worker once took me, the same city where I first caught a bus. Large enough that we can be anonymous, though I didn't ask how they managed to bring Sarah Elizabeth here. She's currently tied up in the bed in the other room, a gag around her mouth.

It's hard to imagine how this day could have gone worse. A man is dead. A girl is kidnapped. And I've learned something horrible, something that explains everything about me.

I *did* come from evil, and I do have a demon inside me—but not because I'm a woman. Not because I have breasts and a vagina. Not even because I like to get spanked by a man I call *Daddy*. No, I'm evil because of what's running through my veins.

His blood.

His genes.

His teachings.

I'm a product of my nature and some very controlling, depraved nurture. It's not something I can ever escape. It's inside. Leader Allen is inside me.

Ivan comes in and washes his hands at the bathroom sink, his back to me.

"What are you going to do with her?"

He turns slightly. "You're awake. How are you feeling?"

"I don't understand why you took her. Won't that only link us to Leader Allen's murder even more?"

"I had room service deliver some fruit and pastries. It's outside on a tray. Let me bring it inside."

"No. *Stop*. I'm not a child. I'm not a little girl you need to feed and spank and put to bed on time. I'm asking you questions, and I deserve answers."

His eyes grow cold. "Fine, you want answers? We took her because she'd have been dead by now if we'd left her. The people there are going to go on a witch hunt when they find him—and she was standing there, holding a shotgun, in shock, wanting to put more bullet holes into a dead man."

I swallow hard because he's right. He may have never met the other men and women in Harmony Hills, but he understands how they work. Just like he understands how I work. We're followers. Sheep. "Is Luca okay?"

"He'll live."

"Why did he take Sarah Elizabeth?"

"We're going to question her. She was close to Leader Allen. She might have heard something."

"I want to be there when you talk to her," I say quickly. I know how intimidating Ivan can be. And I don't think he'd hurt her. He knows that she's innocent even if she knows something. But he can get feral when it comes to the Grand.

I expect him to fight me, but he simply nods. "Come then."

I follow him into the other room.

Sarah Elizabeth's eyes are cloudy as she watches us come in. There's a small dark vial on her nightstand, and I realize that's how they kept her asleep through all this. Did he use it on me too? Or is this sluggishness just part of the shock from this morning?

Ivan settles into a chair in the corner, and I stand awkwardly in the center of the room, trying to figure out where to go. It feels like choosing sides. How they're treating her isn't right. But the Grand needs to be safe again.

Then Luca comes in, and I realize why Ivan is sitting. Luca has a bandage across his stomach and no shirt on. He looks angry. He looks *terrifying* as he pulls a folding knife from his pocket, and I gasp. Sarah Elizabeth gasps too, and squirms away on the bed. With her hands bound behind her back and her ankles tied together, she doesn't get far.

Her gaze is wide now, all sleep drained from them, and so are mine.

Luca grasps her hip, and she goes very still.

I can see her chest rising and falling from beneath the shift. I can see more of her body than I expected to, the shadowed outline of her breasts, the dark circles of her nipples. I never realized how revealing the shifts were. Or maybe it just seemed normal to me back then.

With a rough jerk, Luca slices through the gag around Sarah Elizabeth's mouth. She coughs the fabric onto the bed and then spits into his face, making him laugh. It's a cruel sound, and I realize I've never seen Luca perform his job—as a bodyguard, as an enforcer. He's occasionally been stern with me, but in the end, no matter how much I protested and pretended, I was too obedient to need anything worse. There's blood seeping through the white gauze, making him look savage. He's a wounded animal, and wounded animals lash out.

Sarah Elizabeth has no intention of being obedient. She's glaring at Luca like she'd shoot him again if she were still holding that shotgun. "Let me go."

"Not until you tell me who he sent to fuck with Candy."

Her gaze snaps to mine. "I don't know anything about that. He never told me."

I can see plain as day that she knows the truth. Whatever happened to toughen her up, to make her sad, to make her wield that gun, it didn't manage to make her a better liar. Ivan watches the proceedings from the corner, expression intent but remote.

Luca studies the tip of his knife. "I'm sure he didn't tell you." Then he turns to her, using the knife to wave in her direction, as casually as if he held nothing at all. The metal catches the reflection from the lamp. "But you would have heard something. You lived in the same house as him."

Her eyes are on the knife. "I don't—"

"It's okay," Luca says softly, even more sinister for how reassuring he sounds. "I don't want to hurt you."

He doesn't want to hurt her, but he will.

"I—" Her voice breaks, and fear has replaced the defiance in her eyes. This is the expression Leader Allen would have seen when he taught her how to pray.

It makes me angry. "She said she doesn't know. Leave her alone."

Ivan stands, drawing all our attention. He has a way of commanding a room with just a look. The look he gives me now tells me to shut the hell up. He sits on the edge of the bed, resting a hand on her shoulder.

She freezes, and I can see her pulse jump in her throat.

"Sarah Elizabeth," Ivan says softly, testing out her name. Then he focuses on her. "You have to understand, the Grand is my business. The people who work there, I'm responsible for them. And I should watch over them, shouldn't I?"

Her head nods slowly, eyes never leaving his.

"Someone broke in and left threatening messages. I can't let that go on. I can't let anyone get hurt. Can I?"

She shakes her head no, just as slow. Her eyes are wide. There's still fear, but it's tempered with something else. Understanding. Because Ivan protects me the way Leader Allen never would have protected her.

He leans down and whispers something in her ear. I can't make it out, and I glance at Luca. I expect him to be annoyed that his interrogation was interrupted or maybe just in pure business mode, but he's watching them both with a brooding expression. No, he's watching *her* with a brooding expression.

She swallows hard, looking up at the ceiling. Then at me. "He would talk about you sometimes. He didn't like how...devout I was."

The way she says the words leaves a chill in the air. Every one of us here knows what she means. It has nothing to do with faith.

"He said that you would be better, that he was going to find you, bring you back."

I shiver at the thought of being in that room again. The truth is, I don't believe he could have contained me. I would have gotten out or died trying. I'm different than I was before. Different than Sarah Elizabeth, because she's never been outside. She's never tasted freedom. We were born in captivity, bred and raised to be what he wanted.

"Why didn't he just...take me?" I whisper.

"He said you had demons guarding you."

Ivan raises his eyebrow. Of the names he's been called, *demon* wouldn't be the worst one. And he *was* guarding me. By sending his men to shadow me, he made sure I was safe. Watched over. Even when I ran away, he found me.

Does that make it okay, then, that he doesn't let me leave?

Sarah Elizabeth presses her face almost into the pillow, as if ashamed. "He said he was going to draw her out. He would call her home. And I—I'm so sorry. I wanted him to. I thought when he got you back, he would want you enough that he would leave me alone. I'm sorry."

"Who did he send?" Ivan asks.

"My brother. My brother, Alex. He's never been… never been quite right. Something was always off about him. It was some kind of test Leader Allen sent him on, but the last time he left, he didn't come back."

She's crying by the end of it, sobbing into the pillow. She looks so small curled up on the bed, her wrists and ankles still bound, helpless. Of course she would want him to leave her alone.

"Thank you," Ivan says gently. Then he turns to Luca, "She's all yours."

I follow him into the spacious living area of the suite. "What does that mean? *She's all yours?*"

Ivan pours himself a drink. "It means exactly what it sounds like. He can decide what to do with her. She shot him."

My mouth is open because I can't quite comprehend this. Even as harshly as he's treated me, the way he's dragged me back, the truth is that I always wanted it. This is different. Sarah Elizabeth doesn't want anything Luca would do to her. And she only shot him because she was afraid. "You have to let her go now. She told you what you wanted to know."

He takes a sip from the crystal-cut glass. "I never said

I'd release her."

It enrages me, the way he moves people around like we're dolls in cardboard houses. He has no respect for her—and none for me. In one fast motion, I knock the cup out of his hand. Amber liquid flies through the air and splashes against the cotton-white rug. The crystal glass lands noiselessly on top of it, then rolls onto the marble floor.

Ivan looks at the spilled alcohol, as remote as ever. He takes a step toward me, and I can't help but shrink back. Of course he catches me. He catches me by the chin, his thumb and forefinger holding me still with that single point of contact.

His eyes are frigid as he stares at me. "He wants her. I'm sure you could tell. You always did know how to read men. Allen taught you that much at least."

I flinch. "It's not right," I whisper.

He places a tender kiss on my forehead. "I reward loyalty, little one. You would do well to remember that. Now go stand in the corner until I feel like spanking your pretty ass for spilling my drink."

CHAPTER TWENTY-SEVEN

T HE LAST TIMES I tried to run, the odds were against
me. A lesser man might not have been able to find
me at all—and definitely not as quickly as Ivan. He has a
web that includes dirty cops, kingpins, and good old-
fashioned paid informants.

Of course, that was in Tanglewood.

We aren't there right now. Ivan still has money and
weapons. Not to mention that intimidating, persuasive
charm. He will be able to track me better than most
men, but not like he could back home. No one in this
city even knows who I am. They definitely aren't going
to call him in a twisted version of bros before hos. There
will be no GPS to track, not on a random cab that he'll
never be able to find.

Ivan owns every piece of hay in the haystack that is
Tanglewood, so finding this needle was easy for him. But
here…God, here. We can get lost here. Never to be
found.

Food arrives under silver-domed lids on a wheeled
cart. The bellhop takes one look at Ivan and Luca and
starts sweating. He's gone the second the tip hits his
palm.

The dining table seats exactly four people: Ivan. Luca. Myself. And an angry Sarah Elizabeth with her wrists rubbed red. At least Luca untied her for dinner. I'm not sure I could have even gone along with the false decorum if she had been tied up, hands behind her back while Luca fed her.

As it is, I'm the picture of a flirty hostess. I bring each plate to the table and open it with a flourish. "What would you like to drink?" I ask Ivan.

The look he gives me isn't fooled for a second. I have years of experience fooling men. *Ooh, that's so interesting. I'd love to hear more. You're my favorite client.* They eat that shit up. Ivan just gives me a measured look. The same look all his enemies get, because that's all I am. Not a beloved wife or even a cherished lover. I'm someone to bend to his will. All he's doing now is waiting for me to reveal a weakness.

I smile. "A gin and tonic?"

"A bottle of the wine for the table," he says, and he's definitely suspicious. He would prefer a gin and tonic over merlot any day. He stands and retrieves a bottle from the bar, along with a bottle opener. I sit down, as serene as ever.

He will never see me sweat. Never see me hesitate. He taught me too well for that. Ivan's lessons were very different than Leader Allen's, but they were lessons nonetheless. Leader Allen wanted me to be a subservient, eager follower. Ivan wants me to be a brat, someone he can correct. In the end, what both of them taught me was how to mold myself into whatever a man wants. I do it so well that I think there's nothing left of me. I don't know what I'd be like without a man to please, without someone's command to fight or obey.

It's the woman Ivan wants who sits at the table, submissive except for the private moments where he wants a reason to punish me. He knows me well enough to know it's a game. That knowledge won't help him, though. Not tonight.

Sarah Elizabeth barely touches her food, but I eat everything on my plate. We'll stop for food only when it's convenient, not when we're hungry. I can't tell her that. So we eat in relative silence. The only breaks are when Ivan and Luca murmur over their plans, a limo ride we'll never take and a plane we'll never catch.

Luca doesn't eat at all. He looks fatigued, the lines of his face drawn tight with pain. He won't take any pain medication because that would make him fall asleep. That's fine by me. Now I don't have to worry that I'll overdose him.

My chance comes right after dinner.

"I think I'll have that gin and tonic," Ivan says to me.

"Of course." His wineglass is only half empty. I stand with a demure smile. "Luca?"

His dark gaze flicks to Sarah Elizabeth and then away. "Sure, why not." Then under his breath, "What else would a lowlife thug do but drink."

I can't help but smile at that. It sounds like Sarah Elizabeth has been giving as good as she's getting.

Mixing the drinks only takes a few minutes.

Slipping it in the drinks takes a half second—and a flick of my wrist.

Waiting for the drugs to work...now, that does test my patience. Partly because I know Ivan will understand what I've done in the seconds before he passes out. Of course he would figure it out when he woke up to find me gone anyway, but somehow it's those first seconds before that worry me most. It will be a true betrayal, in the way that running away never was.

The vial had been gone from the nightstand, stowed safely in Ivan's trousers. So I did what I've done for years. I traded my body for what I needed. I let him spank me and fuck me. I gave him a good show, and when he was too sated with climax to notice, when he'd let his guard down the way he could only do for me, I stole the little bottle.

I see the moment recognition passes over his face, cutting through the chemical-induced exhaustion. His gaze flits to mine. There's a slight incline of his head that might be an acknowledgment of what I've done. Or it might be goodbye.

Or it might just be the drugs taking effect, dragging him into unconsciousness. His large body slumps to the floor with a sickening *thud*.

The first thing I do is check his vital signs. *Strong.* The second thing I do is arrange him so that he'll be more comfortable when he wakes up—flat on his back, arms at his side, a pillow from the couch under his head.

Sarah Elizabeth is staring at me, mouth open in shock.

Okay, I guess it would be kind of weird to see two grown men suddenly fall asleep. Especially considering what else happened today. "They're just asleep," I say gently.

"But...but why? I thought you and him were together."

Together. That's one word for what we were. Depraved. Toxic. And beautiful.

"I couldn't let them keep you against your will," I tell her honestly. "Not after what you had been through with Leader Allen. Now come on. We need to cover a lot of ground."

We gather supplies from the hotel room—and from the men themselves. Money from Ivan's wallet, a knife from Luca's pocket. Then we're heading downstairs, hailing a cab. Vanishing into the night. We're five blocks away before Sarah Elizabeth asks the question she's been holding in.

"You could stay behind. He would be mad that you let me go... but he wouldn't hurt you. Would he?"

"Not like you think," I mutter. But he *would* hurt me. "The truth is that I needed to go myself, whether you were here or not. I need to... be my own person."

Not his little one, as much as it hurt to know I'd never hear those softly spoken words again.

By the time Luca and Ivan would regain consciousness in the morning, we are already four hundred miles away. We change clothes and hair colors and accents. Even knowing we've made it safely away, I continue looking over my shoulder. There's both trepidation and hope in those backward glances, but it doesn't matter.

Ivan doesn't find me.

We took the one surefire way I know to disappear—those anonymous gray buses.

And Ivan himself told me where to go.

CHAPTER TWENTY-EIGHT

"**D**ON'T," I SAY, taking the basket away. Beth sticks her tongue out at me but lets me take it from her. She knows she isn't supposed to be lifting heavy things at this point, but she likes to stay active.

"Fine," she says. "If you insist on being a worrywart, I'll go turn that last batch into a pie. They're already going soft."

"Yes, please." I love this girl's baking. Sarah Elizabeth goes by Beth now. She's a happy, playful young woman who bears little resemblance to the timid girl we spirited away all those months ago. However, one thing that remains from her old life is her love of all things domestic. Especially baking. And I can't say that I've complained.

Meanwhile I'm better suited to hard labor, whether that's working a pole or picking peaches from trees. Both leave me exhausted and sore, but the peaches have the added bonus of producing pie.

The ground around the cottage is hard-packed dirt, cool against my bare soles. No hand-sewn linen shoes for me. No stilettos either.

Sarah Elizabeth and I made it all the way to the

coast, to the little countryside town where a boy was abused and neglected. Where he fought with everyone he met. Of course no one knows our connection to this place. Ivan's grandmother passed away a long time ago, her only presence an empty house outside of town.

We rented a little cottage six months ago, servant's lodging for the main house. The landowner never comes here, the local agent told us. I already knew that. This is the one place Ivan will never look for us. The one place he'll never return.

I'm lost to him, but in another way, I'm found. I learn that I can survive on my own. I learn that I miss the relentless, almost reckless passion of a man. And I learn that as much as I miss it, I don't need it after all.

We tell people we're sisters. Picking peaches pays most of the rent. Sarah Elizabeth sells what she bakes to pay for food and other necessities.

It's a good life, a quiet life.

A lonely life.

Physical work means I can fall asleep at night, instead of remembering. Remembering Leader Allen and his last words to me, his revelation. Or was it a confession? Whether he is or isn't my father, he's gone now, forever.

I remember the Grand too, more than I'd like. And Ivan.

So it seems like a mirage when I see him.

I notice the silhouette immediately, a rare break in the sideways sunlight. The shadow turns into a man. And the man turns into...*him*.

The basket turns to lead and slips out of my hand. Peaches tumble to the ground and roll toward him.

I can't see his face, but I recognize the breadth of his shoulders and the lean lines of his hips. I recognize the cut of his suit and the elegant shape of his shoes. I even recognize his hair, the way he forces it down, as if he can control every single strand—but a few in the back always point up if he's had a long day. Like now.

It's a relief to see that he's stayed the same. I feel so different than what I was before. My hair is cut to my shoulders, shorter than it's ever been, and dyed auburn. The sun has brought out freckles on my shoulders, on my chest. The dress I'm wearing is modest and feminine, the ruffle hemline just below my ankles. I am not the girl who cowered in Harmony Hills. I am not the stripper who danced in the Grand.

I am a different person now, a different woman— standing in front of the man I still love.

His eyes are a clear grey, like a winter sky. "Here?" he asks.

In this place where he was tortured and abandoned.

In the place he found beauty and peace.

"Here," I answer.

He nods, just once. "I'd like to have a word with you."

A word. He wants more than a word. He wants to bring me back like I'm a wayward child to be led by the hand. For years I hoped my mother would somehow find me, that she would care enough to come after me. Now

Ivan wants to do that for me, wants to be the caretaker I didn't have, but it's too late. I grew up in between the flashing stage lights and daily spankings. Or maybe I only grew up when I left.

His voice is the one that sounds different. He's still dominant. That is part of his core, not a skin he can slough off. But all the same he sounds…careful. As if this is important.

As if I'm important.

It makes me feel somehow formal. "Would you like to come in?"

"Yes, thank you."

He steps forward, and the light breaks over him, illuminating the patrician nose and high cheekbones, the firm lips and pale eyes. His face still flashes in my mind in the seconds before I come, rubbing myself with my fingers, desperately trying to think of something else—someone else.

He looks exactly as I remembered him. Except for his suit, which is more rumpled and less starched than I've ever seen it, as if he's slept in it overnight. It makes me think of how he would have looked when he first put it on, crisp and handsome. Then he might have thought about our conversations, about the place he swore never to go, and realized where I'd come. Would he have placed a call to the local agent to find out there were two girls renting the cottage on his land? Maybe, but he wouldn't have stopped to confirm. He clearly came straight away, rushed over, desperate.

Something inside me warms at the thought of him hungry to see me.

The door isn't locked. I give it a small nudge, and it swings forward.

At least Sarah Elizabeth is around back. I suppose I should be sending her some kind of warning to run, to hide. I'm in some kind of trance—seeing him here doesn't feel real. I could almost be rubbing myself, in bed, alone, climaxing to the thought of him. That seems more likely.

At least until he brushes by me—solid, warm, with that faint Ivan musk.

Real.

I bring him into the cottage. So much for a warning signal. He obviously found us. If he had planned a smash-and-grab job, he'd already have done so.

The cottage has exposed rafters and whitewashed walls. Lavender dries on the wall, upside down, scenting the air and calming me. This place may be small, but it's mine in a way no place has ever been. Not Harmony Hills. And definitely not the Grand. Those places had belonged to men, and I'd belonged to them too.

Ivan's gray eyes take in every inch of the space, from the overturned crates serving as chairs around a rustic table to the gingham curtain hanging in the middle of the room, half hiding a daybed. At first Sarah Elizabeth and I shared the bedroom, but I moved out so that she could be more comfortable in her final months—and to give her more room when the baby is born.

Nerves flutter in my stomach. What will Ivan think of this house?

His voice is quiet when he speaks. "It's beautiful."

More than quiet, he sounds almost reverent. And I know he doesn't just mean the cottage. He means the life I've built here. He means me.

"Thanks," I say softly, feeling shy.

He clears his throat. "Candace—"

"How is Lola? And the girls?" I have to interrupt him. I can't let him finish. I'm afraid of what he'll say, what he'll ask me. I'm dreading saying no.

A slight nod tells me he knows exactly why I stopped him, but he's letting it go. For now. "Good. We found Bianca."

My heart thumps. It had hurt to leave, even if I'd had no real ties to most of them. Maybe if I could have said goodbye. "Is she okay?"

"She got in deep with a dealer. He was affiliated with Fedor. We're working it out."

Relief and gratitude form a knot in my throat. "Thank you."

His expression turns stark. "I apologize that I let you think I wouldn't help."

He doesn't just mean Bianca. "I always knew you would help me, Ivan. Sometimes the price was just too high."

He's silent a moment. The past whispers between us, spankings and orders and a rough bloody fuck on his bed—somehow beautiful in its brutality.

He nods once, eyes filled with pain. "I'm sorry for that too."

My eyebrows shoot up. He should sound like a stranger, speaking those foreign words. But he doesn't. He apologizes like he does everything else—with the entire force of his will.

"Is that why you came?" I'm the one careful now. I'm the one with something to lose. "To say sorry?"

"That. And other things."

Other things, other things. My imagination can fill in some heartbreaking *other things*. My hands are shaking as I go to the sideboard. "Do you want a drink?"

A pause. "Candace."

I rummage through old, empty liquor bottles, glass soft with dust. There's a bottle of wine I popped when we first moved in. The scent of vinegar makes my nose scrunch up. "Maybe not."

"Candy."

I swallow hard. He never calls me that. I force my hands to my sides, still turned away. "Yes?"

"Would you come sit down?"

Dread. That's what I'm feeling as I turn and face him. And regret. And love. God, is this what love is? It feels like there's a hole in my chest, because there are only two ways this ends. I can be his property or nothing at all.

The cushions have no strength left. They sink as I sit down, pushing me closer to Ivan. Why is this sofa so tiny? It didn't seem that way when Sarah Elizabeth and I would chat late into the night, drinking grape juice instead of stale wine.

I hold myself stiffly, keeping one inch away from him. Without that inch I'll feel his strength, his solidity. Without that inch, I'd have nothing left to hold myself back with. A strip of air is the only thing keeping me safe.

And he knows it. His pale eyes take in my posture, my expression. He looks down at the space between us, and something like defeat crosses his hard features. Then he closes his eyes as if making a decision.

"I've brought you a gift," he says, pulling something from his coat pocket. A slip of paper. "I'm not sure if you want it, but if not, I'm sure my agent in the city can help you dispose of it."

I take the paper as if it might catch fire. It does burn my fingers, just that faint heat from his body. My hands are trembling so much it's hard to read, but then I do. And then the paper goes the same way as the basket, right out of my fingers. Not tumbling and rolling this time. It floats gently to the ground.

The deed to the Grand. That's what he gave me.

I can't—Why would he—

He stands, voice grave, eyes not quite meeting mine. "I'm glad to see you doing so well, Candace. I thought... Well, the country seems to suit you."

Then he's standing, walking away, leaving only the faint impression of expensive fabric and constrained power. I can only stare at the place where he had been, wondering, praying. He'd asked me once, *What do you want then?*

Something to call mine.

Then I'm standing up, saying his name. He's already made it to the door, long strides taken quickly. I have to shout, and it echoes back to me from the walls. He stops walking but doesn't turn. Not until I run toward him, bare feet slapping the floor, graceless and terrified. He's leaving.

And he's leaving his heart behind. It's a hollow man who faces away from me, shoulders tense. He's leaving his heart behind, that's what he's telling me by giving me the Grand. He had a hundred businesses, some of them more lucrative, almost all of them more glamorous than a seedy strip club in the poor part of Tanglewood. It was his heart, and he gave it to me.

"Ivan, wait," I say, catching up to him. "Please."

He turns, only halfway. Listening. Waiting. Hoping? "What is it?"

"Take me with you."

If I'd been hoping for him to take me in his arms, I'd be disappointed. He laughs, a rough sound. "You're happy here, Candace. Stay happy."

"No, I'm—" But I can't lie, not about this. I am happy here, happier than I've ever been. My own place, my own place. My own body to dress and move and touch how I please. It's something I've never had before. "I want to be with you."

He turns to me then, letting me see the ravage on his

face, the utter desolation. "You want a mirage. I'm the man you left behind, little one. That will never change."

My breath catches. *Little one.* "I don't need you to change."

One eyebrow rises, disbelieving. "No? Then why did you leave?"

"Because…" I take a deep breath. "Because I needed to change."

His gaze sweeps over me, cataloging every change. "Maybe you're right. I thought you were beautiful before. Now you look even more beautiful. More than that, you look happy."

He gives me the compliment with such an easy grace, it steals my words. He'd been so closed off before, holding me so tight I couldn't breathe. Now he's giving me the Grand, he's giving me his kindness. He's so open, and with a sinking heart, I realize this might be the end. Only now can he be this open, when he's leaving it all behind. He's finally opening his fist, only for me to realize how much I needed the crush of him, letting me go when I realize how much I want to stay.

My lower lip trembles. Tears fill my eyes. "I'm your little one."

His expression softens a fraction. "I know."

"Then how can you walk away?"

"How can I do anything else? I came here to beg for you back, to tell you I could be different, be *better*. That I wouldn't need to treat you like a little girl. But I can't do any of that." He stalks away two steps and then returns. "Fuck, look at you. You've never looked so happy, so innocent. *And so damn little.*"

I take a step back, away from the fury in his voice. "Is that a bad thing?"

"Yes, it's a fucking—I want you like this all the time. And I want you like this in my goddamn lap while I feed you from my plate and then put you to bed. I can't help wanting it, little one. All I have to do is look at you, and I'm hurting with how much I want you."

I was afraid of his spankings, of his humiliation. I'm still afraid, even though it turns me on. But taking care of me...that's what I want too. He held himself back out of some twisted sense of honor, as if maybe kinky spankings were okay when tenderness was not. "Take care of me, Daddy."

His eyes flash. "Don't fuck with me."

"That's a naughty word."

He reaches for me, hand tangling in my hair. "Daddies use naughty words sometimes. And they do naughty things, don't they?"

"Yes," I say meekly, knowing exactly where this is heading.

He steps forward again. I step back.

"Have you been naughty?" he breathes.

My eyes widen. I don't want to tell him the truth. Not because I can't take the physical pain of a spanking. No, I need that pain—yearn for it in the middle of the night. But I can't take the pain of his coldness, bent over some hard surface while his body is far away, two feet of distance except for his hand against my ass.

I shake my head, lips pressed together.

"No?" he asks, drawing out the word. Another step forward.

Another step back. "I…I don't…"

The backs of my legs hit the daybed, and then I'm falling backward. He's right on top of me, kneeling over me, his presence a delicious shadow blocking out the light. I have a brief thought that the old bed might not support his weight, pure muscle, and so much of it—there's an ominous creak. Then his mouth is on mine, his hands are pressing my wrists above my head, and all thought leaves me.

"Don't hurt me," I whimper.

"Only a little." His voice is dark and seductive, promising I'll like whatever he does. "You'll be a good girl for me, won't you?"

"I wasn't good." I bite my lip, and tears fill my eyes. This is when it will change. This is when *he* will change. "I touched myself. Between my legs."

His lids lower. He puts his free hand on my thigh, slipping between my legs through my skirt. "Here?"

My hands clench into fists. "Umm…a little higher."

He pushes higher, bunching the fabric so it's at the top of my legs. "Was it here?"

My cheeks are burning hot. "Kind of. And kind of… higher."

"Ah," he says gravely. "Did you touch yourself under your panties? Did you make yourself wet, little one?"

"Yes," I whisper. "I knew it was wrong, but I—"

"But you wanted to feel good." His expression seems both sympathetic and severe. "Little girls just want to feel good, don't they? Did you think I'd be mad?"

My eyes widen, and I nod.

He shakes his head slowly, not breaking eye contact. "You didn't have anyone else to make you feel good, but now I'm here. I'm going to be the only one to touch your pretty pussy. Right?"

My breath catches. "Yes, Daddy."

"I'm going to be the only one to make you feel good." He pushes my skirt up, and I press my legs together. He pries them apart. "Don't be afraid."

"It's scary." I don't just mean him touching me or fucking me. I mean trusting him to be my Daddy. I mean letting myself be a little girl. The way he's acting now, tender and open and even a little vulnerable—it feels like a dream. It *was* my dream for so long, and now it's come true.

His face is solemn, gray eyes soft as snow. "I know, little one. You are the bravest little girl I've ever met. You taught me how to be brave too."

Brave? All I've ever done is run away—from Harmony Hills, from the Grand. Ivan is the one who stands his ground, who makes an entire city yield to his demands. "You're not afraid of anything."

Gentle hands pull down my white panties. His eyes darken as he stares between my legs. My skirt is still on, just pushed up around my waist. I try to close my legs, but he's holding them open.

"I was afraid of you," he says softly. "Afraid of how much I wanted you. Afraid I'd corrupt you."

"You didn't," I say because he needs to know. He tried to protect me in his house. I was the one who had to start working at the Grand, to reclaim some kind of power over my life.

He leans down and presses a kiss on my clit, almost chaste. "I did, but not because of who I am or what I do for a living. I corrupted you by giving you pain without the pleasure, by punishing you but never rewarding you. I thought it could keep you safe from my desires, but in the end it only made it worse."

He's opening himself, making himself vulnerable to me, and it only makes me love him more. This is the Daddy I always wanted. This is the Daddy I need.

My sex is pulsing, and I want nothing more than his mouth on me. My legs are shaking where he's holding me open. "So you're not...you're not going to punish me?"

His smile is knowing. "Oh, I'm sure I will. Little girls need to learn how to behave. But I think before that happens...I need to give you a reward."

"You...you do?" I'm breathless now, halfway to begging.

Then his mouth is on me, licking me, teasing me, tying me up in knots. I hold the white iron bars of the daybed as if that can keep me grounded—but nothing can. I'm flying. Then his fingers slip inside me, and I'm falling. He follows me down, flicking his tongue against my clit while I cry out and beg for more, for him to never stop, for him to crash with me, come with me.

For the first time, he listens to me. He releases himself from his suit pants with rough, jerky movements, and then he's inside me, his expression intense, almost pained.

"Don't move."

But I can't help it. I'm rocking underneath him, writhing, my sex clenching around the invasion. "Please."

He makes a low growling sound. "I said don't. Fucking. Move."

My eyes widen, and I grow very still. "I won't."

His gaze softens, even though the tension around his mouth doesn't ease. "I don't want to finish too soon. Not when I've been dreaming about being inside you."

"You dream about me?" I whisper.

"Every damn night." One thrust. Two. "Even before you left."

His cock hits a spot inside me that makes me moan. "Before I…"

His smile is crooked and boyish—completely unlike the Ivan I knew but so much the man I love. This Ivan is letting me see him, all of him. "I tried to keep you safe from me, I really did."

"And now?"

He thrusts in deeper than before, and I flinch. "Now there's no going back."

He opens his shirt, button by button, exposing just a sliver of his dark, broken skin. Then he pulls aside the sides of his shirt, and the full impact of his scars takes my breath away.

He places my hands on his chest. "Do you know what these mean?"

They mean pain. They mean secrets. "Someone hurt you."

He shakes his head. "These were a wall. I was closed off from the world. And you, you kept opening me up. I fought you with everything I had, but in the end, you vanquished me. More than these marks ever did, more than anyone else ever could have."

I make a low sound of sorrow, of grief as my hands move over his broad chest, his abs, feeling the rough texture of him, the marks that couldn't break him.

"You asked me once what makes you different." He holds my wrists still, keeping my hands tight to his body. "This is what makes you special, little one. Countless people have tried to hurt me, to kill me. You were the one to slay me."

"Ivan," I whisper. "Daddy."

His eyes glow with a kind of silver power. He moves my hand so it's directly over his heart, and I feel the thump of it against my palm. "You're here, little one. Forever."

CHAPTER TWENTY-NINE

I KNOW EXACTLY what I'll do with the Grand. Plans that have been forming for years, kept hidden even from myself, are bubbling to the surface. The VIP rooms will have to go, although actual VIP rooms, ones with swanky booths and quiet music, would be wonderful.

For the after-party, of course. There would only be one a night, not a steady stream of single girls onstage. And as for the dancing…let's just say I see a lot more high kicks and bustiers in the show.

I do love the cottage, but it's more like a good friend. The Grand is my forever love.

Like Ivan.

"Did you find Alex?" I ask, holding my breath. The last thing I want to do is have to tell Sarah Elizabeth that her brother has been killed.

Ivan shakes his head. "He's in the wind."

I sigh, one part relief, one part worry.

The only thing keeping me here is Sarah Elizabeth. She's come a long way since leaving Harmony Hills, but I think she's more suited to this cottage than to Tangle-wood. And her baby is due in a few months. I can't leave her here alone. Once the baby is born, she'll need help, support. I don't begrudge her that. I have never been able to shake the guilt over leaving her to Leader Allen, even knowing there was nothing a sixteen-year-old girl could do. And besides, we've become friends.

But every minute spent here is one where I'm not at the Grand. Where I'm not with Ivan.

Now that we're together, now that we're equals, I don't ever want to be apart.

Small sounds are coming from the back room, and I cock my head. What is she doing in there?

Ivan and I head for the door together, hands linked. The cottage is structured in a strange way, with the living quarters in the front and the kitchen in the back. Kind of like the old, grand houses where servants were common, although this place is too small and modest for those.

"Beth?" I call.

No answer. My heart picks up a rhythm.

Ivan's expression hardens, and he pushes me behind him. He nudges the door, and it swings open—revealing Luca and Sarah Elizabeth in a lip-lock, both covered in flour. He's got her backed against the wall, and she doesn't seem to mind. His hands are under her ass, lifting her up. Her hands are in his hair, dusting the black strands with white.

Shock leaves me rooted to the spot, unable to speak.

Her belly isn't exactly large, but it's impossible to miss, a bump from her thin frame. It doesn't seem to bother Luca in the slightest. He presses his big body against hers, rocking his hips in a blunt, insistent motion.

Ivan clears his throat, and Luca's head lifts slightly. He carefully sets Sarah Elizabeth down before turning to face us. It doesn't escape my notice that he blocks her from view, either to give her time to adjust her dress or to protect her from Ivan's wrath.

Well, Ivan doesn't seem mad exactly. More amused. "I told you to keep her occupied."

Luca is unrepentant. "I did."

Ivan turns back to me, his expression hesitant. "We'll have to spend the night here."

He doesn't *quite* phrase it as a question, but I know this is his way of including me. Of letting me take the lead. Of giving me the option to invite him or push him away.

I step close and take his hand again. "We'll make it work. There are some extra bedrolls in the attic."

"And then tomorrow, we'll fly back." Another not question.

Worry tugs at my lips. "Well. I'm not sure I can leave Beth."

She steps out from behind Luca. "I can come with you, if that's what you want. You shouldn't be trapped here because of me."

"No," Luca says. "I'll stay with her."

We all three turn to stare at him. Ivan seems the most shocked. Beth seems scandalized but pleased. As for me? This is the best thing to ever happen to me. Now I can go back to the Grand, back to Ivan, and know that

Sarah Elizabeth is safe.

And plus, I'll never let Luca live this down.

Beth recovers first. "No, it wouldn't be…right."

Pretty much everyone in the room can tell it's a token protest, even Beth. Her cheeks turn red.

"Hmm," I say, tugging Ivan back through the door. "I think we should give these two a chance to talk things out."

Ivan still looks shocked, but he lets me lead him away. "I'm not sure there'll be much talking," he mutters.

It makes me giggle, and I feel exactly like the little girl—like *his* little girl—that I always wanted to be. Light and carefree. Hopeful. "Whatever they're doing, it will probably take… oh, an hour or two. I could show you the orchard."

His lips quirk. "The orchard?"

How does he make normal things sound dirty? "You know…trees, peaches. That orchard."

"Right." He smirks. "Lead the way."

God. "I'm not joking. I've been tending it every day. It's a *lot* of work, almost as tiring as dancing. There's a certain time you have to pick them and—"

I have to stop because Ivan is full-on laughing now, a deep baritone sound that I'm not sure I've ever heard before. I want to be mad at him, but I can't. It's too wonderful seeing him like this, his suit rumpled from the drive, a smile on his face, and lust in his gray eyes. There's nothing left to do but laugh with him while I show him my orchard and all the pretty peaches. I pick one that's ripe and low, feeding it to him and then me, so that both our lips are stained sticky sweet. He lays me down in the shade of a tree, and we do our best to work grass and dirt stains into a ten-thousand-dollar suit.

All my life I've been running, and I'm not going to stop now. Only this time when I run, it's not away from someplace or someone. I'm running *to* someplace, *to* someone. The Grand is my home, and Ivan is my heart. When I am near them, the running turns to dancing. And the dancing is like prayer.

CHAPTER THIRTY

I STAND JUST outside the gates of the Grand, watching dusk set in. Streetlamps carve out sections of the street, flashing loose pavement like diamonds. The alleys are pitch black—anyone could be happening in them. Anything *is* happening in them. Men know better than to approach me. Ivan's reputation—and my own—are well known. But I don't fool myself that I'm safe in this city just because I love it. It's like loving a volcano, knowing one day you'll get burned.

A hand circles my wrist, and I jump.

When I turn, my heart thumps faster. *Ivan.* "You came."

He leans in to place a kiss on my forehead, and I close my eyes. It feels so right—the faint heat of him, his breath. I shiver.

"Of course," he says simply. This is a big night for the Grand. A big night for me. We've had a soft open for weeks now, but this is the official opening. Ivan has been incredibly busy growing his other businesses now that he isn't spending all of his time at the Grand, but he makes sure to attend one show a week. And he swore he wouldn't miss this one.

PRETTY WHEN YOU CRY

PRETTY WHEN YOU CRY

On impulse, I wrap my arms around him. "Thank you."

He drops his chin on my hair. "You know you shouldn't be out here without West."

West is my new personal bodyguard. Now that Luca is with Sarah Elizabeth, he needed someone else to trust with me—and of course it's the boy scout. "He's helping inside," I say, brushing over the fact that I ordered him to and then slipped away. He will not be pleased. "And besides, you're here now."

He raises one eyebrow, not amused. "Am I?"

Rhetorical questions mean I'm in trouble. To distract him I take a step back and finger the fine, blush-colored material of my dress. It's constructed from layers that are like petals, and I twirl for maximum effect. It only blooms when I dance.

"What do you think?" I ask. One of the advantages of being a former stripper is that I can execute that move in sparkly gold Louboutin's on cobblestone. "I look like a flower."

He's sufficiently distracted, eyes sweeping down to the floor. "A flower with incredible legs," he mutters.

I bite my lip and step close. Some women seem to grow taller when their man appreciates them, gaining confidence—and that's a beautiful thing. But me, I'm the opposite. I already have a surplus of confidence, of swagger. Only with Ivan can I let myself be small. I curl into him, just a little. Soon I'll have to return to the crowd, to be the social butterfly, the hostess, but for now

I let myself be *his*.

I play with the lapel of his jacket. "Are you going to take me down to the basement after?"

"Why? Have you been a bad girl?"

"Nooo," I say, hoping he doesn't ask for details, knowing he will. "I thought you could reward me for working so hard."

"Ah," he says in that short, knowing way of his. "Of course good girls should be rewarded. Tell me, little one. Did you eat dinner tonight?"

Shit. "Well… no. But I was thinking I could grab some hors d'ourves after I dance. My tummy is too twisted to eat anyway."

"What about lunch?" he asks without missing a beat.

If I tell him the truth, he'll be so mad. I could see him dragging me into the kitchens and standing over me until I ate something. "Yes," I lie.

He studies me for a moment. Then he says, "All right. Go be beautiful and gracious and powerful. And when you are done, I will take you down to the basement."

I shiver. "Please, Daddy."

His mouth is next to my ear when he whispers, "I'll have to punish you for that lie, little one."

A squeak of alarm escapes me, but then West appears at the gate, looking haggard. Ivan sends him a disapproving look. Poor West. I do keep him on his toes. Speaking of which, I hope Sarah Elizabeth is keeping Luca on his toes. Now that I think about it, I'm sure she is.

We return to the courtyard where the crowd has gathered to watch the unveiling. The doors of the Grand are open, and people are packed all the way inside, looking out. They hold champagne flutes and martini glasses. The men are impeccable in their tuxes and slicked back hair—the same men who once frequented the Grand as a strip club. The women on their arms are dressed in Armani and Valentino, every shade of orange and pink and gold. They love to whisper about the salacious past of the Grand even while they drop a thousand dollars on a ticket.

In the center of it all is the fountain. It's never worked the entire time I've been here. The statue at the top has been broken since I got here, and it's gotten smashed even worse since then. The trough collects dry leaves and dirt.

Now it's covered by yards and yards of black silk.

"Thank you all for coming," I tell everyone. "The Grand has been my dream, my home. It's been my deepest desire, and I'm thrilled tonight to share it with you all."

The eyes of the crowd shine with lust. The men want my body. Some of the women want it too. They're covetous and cruel and absolutely beautiful.

"Without further delay, please let me present to you all an incredible artist and lovely young woman."

Clara stands up, looking nervous and brave. She gives a speech about this commission—her first major piece to be in public. Her sister, Honor, is in the audience. Her dark eyes shine with pride as she watches her younger sister speak. Honor is wearing a black sheath and simple gold string necklace. She looks sophisticated and demure. No one would guess from looking at her that she had the most flawless pole technique I've ever seen.

Lola is beside her, with Blue's arms wrapped around her waist. He doesn't leave her side when he can help it, and especially not here, when Sarah Elizabeth's brother, Alex, has never been caught. He hasn't struck again either, so we're hoping he gave up his horrible crusade and went somewhere far away—away from Harmony Hills and away from us.

When Clara is finished speaking, she nods to the men on either side of the fountain. They're bouncers. High class bouncers, and they fill out their tuxes so nicely. They reach down and pull the black silk away, unveiling the new statue atop the fountain.

An angel stands on top of the fountain. Her wings are spread wide, strong and capable of carrying her anywhere. One wing is slightly crooked, like a bird who's injured her wing. But she still stands tall, chin held high. Her hair falls in loose waves, the kind of texture you get after being out at sea, salt and water spray leaving its mark. And her eyes—the angels eyes are what you remember most. They're strong and fierce, so deter-mined. This isn't an angel to pray or bless you. This is a warrior, one who knows the evils of the world and fight them every day.

The crowd gasps, torn between genuine appreciation

and their jaded addiction to criticism. They applaud Clara and demand, simply *demand,* that she create custom pieces for them all. She'll be very busy, assuming she wants to create ego centerpieces for cunning rich people.

Ivan squeezes my hand. "It's lovely."

I give him a wink. "Wait until you see the show."

Those lovely gray eyes widen. I don't dance very often, not onstage, focusing instead on the choreography, the staging, and the front of the house. Not to mention the number crunching on the backend. It keeps me busy, but I wanted to be part of this night, of this show. I wanted this to be a true transition from what the Grand had been to what it has become. That means never forgetting where it came from, just like I can never forget. There are scars on the Grand, in the walls themselves. Just like there are scars on Ivan's body. They tell a story about where it's been—and about where it's going.

✧　✧　✧

IT'S A RUSH out onstage again, the lights, the feeling of flying. I dance with the other girls in formation through our opening act and then wait backstage for a few of the sets.

Then it's my turn.

My dance is a blend of stripper moves and burlesque, both crude and sultry, both fierce and whimsical. It's an ode to the past, this song. And hope for the future. When I'm done, I'm breathless, weightless.

I'm almost euphoric as I head down the familiar hallway and into the dressing room. It had to be expanded to accommodate the full company of dancers. They're bustling about, getting ready for the show. Some of them give me a hug and kiss, congratulating me on my performance, but I'm careful not to smudge their makeup.

Then I see Honor at my vanity, with Lola at her side. Blue is there, looking severe.

My heart drops. All I can think about is Alex. Did he do something else? Leave more blood? *Hurt someone?*

"What's wrong?" I manage to ask over the knot in my throat.

"It's Clara," Honor says. "She was supposed to sit with us, but when we all took our seats, she wasn't there. She isn't anywhere."

Oh God. There's a steel band around my chest, and I can't breathe. If anything happened to Clara, I don't know what I would do. She's too sweet for this place. Too innocent. Why did I ever ask her to make a sculpture for us?

"She probably just got a ride with some friends," Lola says, but her big brown eyes are filled with worry. We all know that Clara is careful, thoughtful. She would have at least told her sister she was leaving.

Kip appears, looking out of breath. "We searched the perimeter of the Grand, but we're going to go wider."

In other words, he hasn't found her.

I squeeze Honor's hand. "I'm sure she'll turn up just fine, and then you'll be able to ground her for life."

Honor gives me a wan smile. "She's eighteen now. I can't ground her at all."

A grown woman. She's seen so much, but it never changed her. It never hardened her. Which means she doesn't have any defenses against the dark side of Tanglewood. Definitely none against Alex and the perverted teachings of Harmony Hills. Now I understand Ivan's murderous rage. If he hurt one silky blonde hair on her head…

My phone lights up on my vanity, and suspicion makes my eyes narrow. I manage to keep a blank expression as I grab it from the small table and move aside. They'll think I'm only checking my messages or maybe calling her. Presumably they've tried and gone to voicemail.

Sure enough, there's a text. *Sorry*, it says.

Where are you?? Honor is freaking out.

Don't tell her I talked to you. Pls.

Umm… why? She's going to have a heart attack.

You owe me.

Crap, she's right. I do owe her after she helped me out that night. I hate having to keep Honor in the dark though. I hate being in the dark, because I don't know what's happening either. At least, wherever she is, she has her phone and the presence of mind to text me.

I type again. *Are you safe?*

For now.

I think I'm going to strangle that girl. Only after

Honor has a go of it, of course. But maybe every girl needs a little rebellion. She might need it more than most, the way Honor has protected her—overprotected her. After their rough beginning, it's understandable that her older sister wanted to hold her tightly. Maybe a little too tight.

At least she isn't taking a gray bus out of town, never to be heard from again. Well, I'm pretty sure she's not doing that.

Stay that way or I'll hurt you, I type before shutting off the screen.

My mind is racing, trying to think of how I can keep Honor calm without actually telling her anything. Okay, that is pretty impossible.

Ivan appears in the door, where I've seen him so many times. He doesn't come inside, just gestures for me to come out. I can tell by his dire expression that he's heard Clara is missing. In the hallway, I burrow myself into his side, needing to feel his solidity, his strength.

"Do you know where she is?" he asks, so softly I barely can hear him.

I shake my head without looking at him. "But she said she's okay."

He gives a faint nod. "That's enough for now."

Enough for now. Yes. I can trust her that much. God knows, she trusted me much more than that. I have to hope she knows what she's doing, because I love her like a sister.

I love Honor like a sister. Lola too. I have an entire

family here, built with every swing of the pole, every rough customer thrown out. For so long after I left Harmony Hills, I felt the loneliness like physical pain. But these girls are my family.

The Grand is my home, just like I told a crowd full of beautiful strangers tonight.

And this man is my heart.

Ivan watches me with quicksilver eyes. "To the basement, little one."

He calls to me, and I follow him down, into the heat of him, the depths of him, burned and made new again. He takes my desire and turns it around, turns it into sweetness. He takes my kindness, my love, and warps it into lust. And each time he twists me, I'm bound a little closer to him, tied a little tighter. There is nothing that could break us now.

Every love story is a knot, and ours is threaded with steel.

He follows me down the metal stairs, and I whirl in the dank grey space, a flash of color, a bloom. "Where do you want me, Daddy?"

He sits at the high-back chair and pats his lap. I start to climb onto him, but he shakes his head. "Bend over, little one."

I drape myself over him instead. His thighs are warm and unyielding against my front, caressing my breasts. He pushes up my skirt, and I hear his breath catch at what he sees.

My lace panties are torn away. They land on the concrete, a pile of pink scraps.

He found me lost, alone, and helpless—and gave me a place to call mine. This basement, this building. The space where he watches me, both of us held by our own dark desires, in these moments before he gives me my reward.

We are made of the same thing, he and I. Of sin and hope, of power and pleasure.

We were made to dream.

Thank You

Thank you for reading Pretty When You Cry. I hope you loved Ivan and Candy's story!

The next couple in the Stripped series is Giovanni and Clara. Hold You Against Me comes out in early 2016. Make sure you sign up for my newsletter so you can find out when it releases!

The previous couple in the Stripped series is Blue and Lola. You can read their story in the novel Better When It Hurts and sexy follow up novella Even Better.

If you're new to the series, meet Giovanni and Clara for free in the prequel novella Tough Love. Then read the scorching hot and darkly mysterious Love the Way You Lie with Kip and Honor.

You can also join my Facebook group, Skye Warren's Dark Room, to discuss the Stripped series and my other books!

I appreciate your help in spreading the word, including telling a friend. Reviews help readers find books! Please leave a review on your favorite book site.

Pretty When You Cry is dark, dangerous, and twisted. If you loved this, you will probably also love Wanderlust. Turn the page to read an excerpt…

EXCERPT FROM WANDERLUST

I FELT TINY out here. Would it always be this way now that I was free? Our seclusion at home had provided more than security. An inflated sense of pride, diminishing the grand scheme of things to raise our own importance. On this deserted sidewalk in the middle of nowhere, it was clear how very insignificant I was. No one even knew I was here. No one would care.

When I rounded the corner, I saw that the lights in the gas station were off. Frowning, I tried the door, but it was locked. It seemed surreal for a moment, as if maybe it had never been open at all, as if this were all a dream.

Unease trickled through me, but then I turned and caught site of the sunset. It glowed in a symphony of colors, the purples and oranges and blues all blending together in a gorgeous tableau. There was no beauty like this in the small but smoggy city where I had come from, the skyline barely visible from the tree in our backyard. This sky didn't even look real, so vibrant, almost blinding, as if I had lived my whole life in black and white and suddenly found color.

I put my hand to my forehead, just staring in awe.

My God, was this what I'd been missing? What else

was out there, unimagined?

I considered going back for my camera but for once I didn't want to capture this on film. Part of my dependence on photography had been because I never knew when I'd get to see something again, didn't know when I'd get to go outside again. I was a miser with each image, carefully secreting them into my digital pockets. But now I had forever in the outside world. I could breathe in the colors, practically smell the vibrancy in the air.

A sort of exuberant laugh escaped me, relief and excitement at once. Feeling joyful, I glanced toward the neat row of semi-trucks to the side. Their engines were silent, the night air still. The only disturbance: a man leaned against the side of one, the wispy white smoke from his cigarette curling upward. His face was shrouded in darkness.

My smile faded. I couldn't see his expression, but some warning bell inside me set off. I sensed his alertness despite the casual stance of his body. His gaze felt hot on my skin. While I'd been watching the sunset, he'd been watching me.

When he suddenly straightened, I tensed. Where a second ago I'd felt free, now my mother's warnings came rushing back, overwhelming me. Would he come for me? Hurt me, attack me? It would only take a few minutes to run back to my room—could I beat him there? But all he did was raise his hand, waving me around the side of the building. I circled hesitantly and found another entrance, this one to a diner.

Hesitantly, I waved my thanks. After a moment, he nodded back.

"Paranoid," I chastised myself.

The diner was wrapped with metal, a retro look that was probably original. Uneven metal shutters shaded the green windows, where an OPEN sign flickered.

Inside, turquoise booths and brown tables lined the walls. A waitress behind the counter looked up from her magazine. Her hair was a dirty blonde, darker than mine, pulled into a knot. A thick layer of caked powder and red lipstick were still in place, but her eyes were bloodshot, tired.

"I heard we got a boarder," she said, nodding to me. "First one of the year."

I blinked. It was a cool April night. If I was the first one of the year, then that was a long time to go without boarders.

"What about all the trucks outside?"

"Oh, they sleep in their cabs. Those fancy new leather seats are probably more comfortable than those old mattresses filled with God-knows-what." She laughed at her own joke, revealing a straight line of grayish teeth.

I managed a brittle smile then ducked into one of the booths.

She sidled over with a notepad and pen.

"We don't usually see girls as pretty as you around here. Especially alone. You don't got nobody to look after you?"

The words were spoken in accusation, turning a compliment into a warning.

"Just passing through," I said.

She snorted. "Aren't we all? Okay, darlin', what'll it be?"

Under her flat gaze, I turned the sticky pages of the menu, ignoring the stale smells that wafted up from it. Somehow the breakfast food seemed safest. I hoped it would be easier to avoid food poisoning with pancakes than a steak.

After the waitress took my order, I waited, tapping my fingers on the vinyl tabletop to an erratic beat. I was a little nervous—jittery, although there was no reason to be. Everyone had been nice. Not exactly welcoming, but then I was a stranger. Had I expected to make friends with the first people I met?

Yes, I admitted to myself, somewhat sheepishly. I had rejected my mother's view that everyone was out to get me, but neither was everyone out to help me. I would do well to retain some of the wariness she'd instilled in me. A remote truck stop wasn't the place to meet people, to make lasting relationships. That would be later, once I had started my job. No, even later than that, when I'd saved up enough to reach Niagara Falls. Then I could relax.

When my food came, I savored the sickly sweet syrup that saturated my pancakes. It would rot my teeth, my mother would have said. Well, she wasn't here. A small rebellion, but satisfying and delicious.

The bell over the door rang, and I glanced up to see a man come in. His tan T-shirt hung loose while jeans hugged his long legs. He was large, strong—and otherwise unremarkable. He might have come from any one of those eighteen-wheelers out there, but somehow I knew he'd been the one watching me.

His face had been in the shadows then, but now I could see he had a square jaw darkened with stubble and lips quirked up at the side. Even those strong features paled against the bright intensity of his eyes, both tragic and terrifying. So brown and deep that I could fall into them. The scary part was the way he stared—insolently. Possessively, as if he had a right to look at me, straight in my eyes and down my neckline to peruse my body.

I suddenly felt uncomfortable in this dress, as if it exposed too much. I wished I hadn't changed clothes. More disturbing, I wished I had listened to my mother. I looked back down at my pancakes, but my stomach felt stretched full, clenched tight around the sticky mass I'd already eaten.

I wanted to get up and leave, but the waitress wasn't here and I had to pay the bill. More than that, it would be silly to run away just because a man looked at me. That was exactly what my mom would do.

Back when we still left the house, someone would just glance at her sideways in the grocery store. Then we'd flee to the car where she'd do breathing exercises before she could drive us home. I was trying to escape that. I *had* escaped that. I wouldn't go back now just because a man with pretty eyes checked me out.

Still, it was unnerving. When I peeked at him from beneath my lashes, I met his steady gaze. He'd seated himself so he had a direct line of vision to me. Shouldn't he be more circumspect? But then, I wouldn't know what was normal. I was clueless when it came to public interaction. So I bowed my head and poked at the soggy pancakes.

Once the waitress gave me the bill, I'd leave. Simple enough. Easy, for someone who wasn't paranoid or crazy. And I wasn't—that was my mother, not me. I could do this.

When the waitress came out, she went straight to his table. I drew little circles in the brown syrup just to keep my eyes off them. I couldn't hear their conversation, but I assumed he was ordering his meal.

Finally, the waitress approached my table, wearing a more reserved expression than she had before. Almost cautious. I didn't fully understand it, but I felt a flutter of nerves in my full stomach.

She paused as if thinking of the right words. Or maybe wishing she didn't have to say them. "The man over there has paid for your meal. He'd like to join you."

I blinked, not really understanding. The gentleness of her voice unnerved me. More than guilt—pity.

"I'm sorry." I fumbled with the words. "I've already eaten. I'm done."

"You have food left on your plate. Doesn't matter how much you want to eat anyway." She paused and then carefully strung each word along the sentence. "He requests the pleasure of your company."

My heart sped up, the first stirrings of fear.

I supposed I should feel flattered, and I did in a way. He was a handsome man, and he'd noticed me. Of course, I was the only woman around besides the waitress, so it wasn't a huge accomplishment. But I wasn't prepared for fielding this kind of request. Was this a common thing, to pay for another woman's meal?

It was a given that I should say no. Whatever he wanted from me, I couldn't give him, so it was only a question of letting him down nicely.

"Please tell him thank you for the offer. I appreciate it, I do. But you see, I really am finished with my meal and pretty tired, so I'm afraid it won't be possible for him to join me. Or to pay for my meal. In fact, I'd like the check, please."

Her lips firmed. Little lines appeared between her brows, and with a sinking feeling I recognized something else: fear.

"Look, I know you aren't from around here, but that there is Hunter Bryant." When I didn't react to the name, her frown deepened. "Here's a little advice from one woman to another. There are some men you just don't say no to. Didn't your mama ever warn you about men like that?"

Want to read more? Wanderlust is available now at Amazon.com, iBooks, BarnesAndNoble.com and other retailers.

OTHER BOOKS BY SKYE WARREN

Standalone Dark Romance
Wanderlust
On the Way Home
His for Christmas
Hear Me
Take the Heat

Stripped series
Tough Love (prequel)
Love the Way You Lie
Better When It Hurts
Even Better
Pretty When You Cry

Chicago Underground series
Rough
Hard
Fierce
Wild
Dirty
Secret
Sweet

Criminals and Captives series

Prisoner

Dark Nights series

Keep Me Safe

Trust in Me

Don't Let Go

Dark Nights Boxed Set

The Beauty series

Beauty Touched the Beast

Beneath the Beauty

Broken Beauty

Beauty Becomes You

The Beauty Series Compilation

Loving the Beauty: A Beauty Epilogue

ABOUT THE AUTHOR

Skye Warren is the New York Times and USA Today Bestselling author of dark romance. Her books are raw, sexual and perversely romantic.

Sign up for Skye's newsletter:
www.skyewarren.com/newsletter

Like Skye Warren on Facebook:
facebook.com/skyewarren

Join Skye Warren's Dark Room reader group:
skyewarren.com/darkroom

Follow Skye Warren on Twitter:
twitter.com/skye_warren

Visit Skye's website for her current booklist:
www.skyewarren.com

COPYRIGHT

Pretty When You Cry © 2015 by Skye Warren
Print Edition

Cover design by Book Beautiful
Cover photograph by Sara Eirew
Formatting by BB eBooks

26588211R00156

Made in the USA
Middletown, DE
02 December 2015